# BETWEEN CHRISTMAS AND

# Romance

Christmas Mountain Series Book 7

*A Sweet Holiday Romance*

by
*USA TODAY* Bestselling Author
**SHANNA HATFIELD**

# *Between Christmas and Romance*

Cover Design by For the Muse Design

*To those who love small town life...*

# *Books by Shanna Hatfield*

## FICTION

## *Chapter One*

Steam redolent with the scents of cinnamon, cloves, apples, and a hint of citrus wafted in delicious, feathery plumes from the mug I held in my chilled fingers.

My head dipped closer to the mug emblazoned with my store logo and I breathed deeply of the fragrance. Content, I sighed and took a sip, letting the warm, sweet liquid warm me from the inside out.

Hemingway, my contrary cat, filled the quiet of the November morning with loud purrs as he curled up on the chair beside me. If I didn't know better, I'd assume the finicky feline enjoyed the pleasing aroma, too.

"What do you think, Hemi? Hmm? Is it time to go downstairs and open the shop?"

The cat swished his tail but didn't open his eyes or show any interest in moving from the overstuffed chair that had become our favorite spot to begin and end the day.

Back in March, I'd been dropping the trash in the dumpster in the alley when I noticed the cat. Fully grown, the black-striped tabby was all tawny fur and bones. Although he was standoffish, it didn't take long to win him over. Before I knew it, he'd become the store's mascot.

I used to feel sorry for him, but now I'm just glad for his company, even if he can be a little imperious at times.

My hand gently stroked across the soft fur of his back and his purring increased in volume. "I'll feed you breakfast," I offered as an incentive to get him up and moving.

Green eyes blinked at me as the cat lazily stretched then hopped down and headed toward my apartment door. He looked over his shoulder with a scowl, as though I should have immediately followed.

"You're getting bossier by the day, Hemi." I picked up my cell phone and a set of keys, tucking them inside the pockets of my long cardigan sweater then opened the door. The cat marched out and around the bookcase that hid the entrance to our private domain.

At the last minute, I remembered my glasses and snatched them from the pie crust table by the door, settling them on top of my head. I walked around the bookcase then pulled a wooden panel shut. It gave the appearance of a wall and kept anyone from finding my apartment door. A girl couldn't be too careful about protecting her privacy and I guarded mine with extreme diligence.

Hemi meowed and minced his way down the winding stairs, but I remained where I was at the top of the landing, looking out over my business. Since purchasing the bookstore last year, I'd worked hard to change it in a subtle way that wouldn't upset or offend the residents of Christmas Mountain, my Montana hometown.

After all, Rudolph's Reads has been an institution in Christmas Mountain for what seems like forever. It was certainly a place of refuge for me during the challenging years of my childhood.

When Mr. Abernathy, the previous owner, mentioned his plans to retire, I jumped at the opportunity to purchase the business. I needed a place of escape and I couldn't think of anywhere better than the town where I spent my growing up years.

With another sip of my spicy tea, I took one more glance over the rough-hewn timbers, shelves bursting with books, cozy seating areas, and the island in the midst of it all that served as the checkout counter and my desk. Above it, hanging from the ceiling, was a life-sized stuffed reindeer with a red nose holding a colorful copy of *Twas the Night Before Christmas*, as though he read the story. A balcony encircled the second floor of the store, leaving the center open, except for Rudolph and his book. And of course, there was my apartment tucked in the back, hidden behind a sturdy bookcase.

I drew in a long breath, savoring the scent of the tea in my left hand as well as the smell of books, old wood, and lemon oil. I used the oil faithfully to keep all the shelves, beams, and furniture polished to a high shine.

Hemi leaped onto the checkout counter and glowered at me with a demanding meow.

"I'm coming, your highness." With one last look around the store, I sauntered down the stairs, set the mug of tea near the cash register, then made my way down the back hallway to the storage room where I kept Hemi's food and water bowl. He had a big, fluffy bed there, along with a litter box, and a collection of toys that he rarely even looked at let alone used.

I cracked open the back door and he darted outside while I dumped cat food into his bowl and refilled his water dish. The cold caused me to shiver as I waited for the cat, but I breathed deeply. I appreciated the combined smells of wood smoke, pine trees, and fresh mountain air.

Thankfully, Hemi didn't tarry long in the great outdoors. He rushed back in and made a beeline for his food. The sound of his crunching drew out my smile as I closed the door and locked it, then washed my hands at the sink in the corner.

On my way out front, I stopped to make sure the bathroom was clean and stocked with necessities for my customers. Assured everything was in good order, I continued to the checkout counter, turned on my computer, checked the connection of the cash register, and sipped my rapidly cooling tea.

I'd just walked over to the door to unlock it when I felt something brush against my leg. A glance down confirmed Hemi did his best to cover my black tights with fur.

"Must you do that, Hemi?"

His innocent look won me over, like it always did. I bent down and gave him several good scratches along his back and in the spot behind his right ear that caused his purring to sound like a revving engine before I unlocked the door and turned the closed sign around to open.

Today, I planned to design my holiday displays between taking care of customers and answering the phone. I'd already cleared a section near the front of the store, between the romance and travel sections, where I'd started arranging holiday books and gift items.

I could have focused solely on that, but my two part-time employees were unavailable to watch the store today.

Marilyn, a sweet grandmother of five, came to me not long after I purchased the store. Desperate for a job that would get her out of the house, the poor woman claimed her husband's retirement had been one of the worst things that ever happened to her. The man spent all his time at home offering suggestions on how she could improve her housekeeping efficiency or watching golf, which Marilyn despised. She needed time away from him to keep from threatening to leave him if he didn't return to work.

Karen had two rambunctious boys, ages three and two, and claimed working at the store a few days a week was the only thing that kept her sanity intact. Between the two of them, I had help from ten to two every weekday.

But Marilyn had gone to her daughter's place in Bozeman for the Thanksgiving holiday and wouldn't be back until Tuesday. Karen's boys were both sick so she didn't feel right leaving them with her mother-in-law, who usually babysat for her on Wednesdays and Fridays. Karen promised to be at the store Friday morning bright and early to help with the Black Friday shoppers, though.

The two high school students who worked every Saturday and alternating afternoons from three until six would be available to lend a hand, too. I asked both Aiden and Josie to come in this afternoon so they could help me decorate the store. We'd get the artificial Christmas tree set up and make a big dent in creating holiday displays.

Gaze narrowed, I tipped my head to the right and envisioned how a Christmas tree would look at the back of the holiday display with white lights twinkling and traditional red plaid ribbons streaming around the branches.

"Perfect," I whispered. "It will look perfect."

It had been far too many years since I'd been able to celebrate Christmas in a truly meaningful way. Not until I returned to Christmas Mountain last year. It had been like a weight lifted off my shoulders the moment I drove into town.

Home.

Christmas Mountain was home and I belonged here.

I was settled in as a business owner, even if I

did prefer to hide out in my store rather than socialize. Friends from my school days occasionally talked me into outings. There were seven of us who had shared a special friendship thanks to our music teacher, Ms. King. Moments spent with Ashley, Morgan, Lexi, Emma, Faith, Joy, and my favorite teacher would always be sweet memories I cherished. Due to nothing but my own stubbornness, I'd lost touch with all of them until I moved back last year and reconnected with them. Now, the girls made sure I left the store on occasion and engaged in a little fun from time to time. And I'd renewed a close friendship with Joy that brought me a great deal of happiness.

With my heart full of happiness at the prospect of another fabulous day spent doing something I greatly enjoyed, I made a pot of coffee, set out more foam cups and napkins near the pot, then flipped on the radio to a station that filled the store with easy listening music. Come Friday morning, I'd play non-stop Christmas music until New Year's Day.

I'm aware Christmas music can drive some people mad, but I love it. I cherish the old carols. I treasure the songs made popular during the war years. There are even a number of new Christmas tunes I adore. And I plan to play them all.

Thoughts of Christmas songs caused me to hum a familiar carol as I gave the counter a quick once-over with a dust cloth before I plopped into the red leather high-backed office chair at my computer. I'd just finished replying to emails and placing an order for books when the bell above the door jangled.

Mr. Abernathy walked inside and headed

straight for the coffee. It wasn't until he'd taken a sip that he casually made his way over to the counter. Since I purchased the store, this had become a routine we both enjoyed every Tuesday and Thursday.

Like clockwork, he arrived at half past nine to drink coffee and jokingly tell me at least one way I could do a better job of keeping up the store his grandmother started. I'd feign offense, or tell him to mind his own business, then we'd talk about the latest new releases and anything exciting taking place in the book world or the community.

If it wasn't for Mr. Abernathy, I don't know what I would have done, both as a child and when I returned to Christmas Mountain. He'd saved me from myself in my younger years, and from things I preferred not to think about more recently.

"You do know shoppers will be in here wanting full blown holiday cheer bright and early Friday morning, don't you, Miss Bennett?" he asked as he leaned an elbow on the counter and looked around the store.

"I certainly do. That's why I decided to take down the reindeer and put up a big beach display," I teased, waiting for his reaction.

He choked on his coffee and whipped his head around to glare at me instead of studying the festive Christmas travel mugs I'd already stocked on a nearby shelf.

"You wouldn't dare remove Rudolph." Everyone in town knew the reindeer hanging above the cash register was like an institution, an unchangeable tradition. It would take someone bigger and braver than me to rid the store of the reindeer. Besides, with a name like Carol and a passion for all things Christmas, the last thing on my mind was replacing old Rudy.

"Try me." I grinned at Mr. Abernathy.

He smiled and slurped his coffee.

Mr. Abernathy could only be described as a strange little man. I had no idea how tall he claimed to be, but since I was five-eleven, I guessed him to be a good six inches shorter. He was thin, pale, with a mustache that reminded me of Mr. Spacely, the anti-hero from *The Jetson's* cartoons. But Mr. Abernathy was kind. At least if you got past his bookish exterior to the softie he really was at heart.

I first discovered the haven of Rudolph's Reads when I was eight. I'd ducked inside to avoid my mother as she searched all over town for me and lost myself in the rows of books.

Mr. Abernathy had scowled and warned me not to touch anything I didn't plan to buy, but I couldn't resist walking through the store, inhaling the scents of books and adventures. When I left, he gave me what was almost a smile. The next time I ventured in, he told me the same thing, but showed me a section of used books at the back of his store and suggested several I might enjoy. A comfy sitting area in an alcove tucked beyond the view of shoppers became my spot. I would curl up there and read to my heart's content. Mr. Abernathy even let me read new books, as long as I didn't damage the books or crack the spine. I was fifteen when I gathered the courage to ask him about a job. He hired me on the spot and I worked evenings and weekends, at least when my mother didn't have other plans.

He and Ms. King are the reasons I somehow survived my childhood.

"Do you need help with the tree?" Mr. Abernathy asked after he took another long drink of the coffee.

"Aiden and Josie will help. Between the three of us, we should be able to manage, but thanks for the offer. Will you come in Friday and let me know what you think?"

He shook his head. "The last place you'll find me is in a store on Black Friday." He gave me an observant glance. "Unless you need help."

"I've got it covered. Why don't you come in Saturday, then?"

"I'll do that, Carol." He finished his coffee and tossed the cup in the garbage can by the door. "You know how to call me if you do need help."

"I do, Mr. Abernathy. Thank you." I watched as he walked outside and continued on his way, hunching into his coat in the cold air. Sometimes, I wondered if he was as lonely as I felt. As far as I knew, he'd never been married and had lived alone all these years. He had to be nearing his eighties. He'd seemed ancient the first time I met him and that was many years ago.

"Is that going to be me in fifty years, Hemi?" I asked the cat as he sauntered in from the hallway and sat near the spinning rack of greeting cards, licking his front paws. "I'll be the crazy cat woman who has a store full of books, cats running amuck, and no life."

About to depress myself with my maudlin musings, I shifted my focus back to the Christmas display. Thoughts of the upcoming holidays were sure to brighten my mood. I leaned forward and stared at the Christmas display space. I wanted it to be more than just a tree, holiday books, and a few gift items. I wanted people to walk in and be awed.

Inspired, I looked up several ideas on my computer between customers. At a lull between shoppers, I hopped up and hurried to the storage room where shelves on one wall held a variety of decorations Mr. Abernathy had collected over the years. The new lights and ornaments I ordered were there, along with the ribbon I planned to toss like confetti around the displays. I was going to need more lights, garlands, ribbon, and a crate of candy canes if I wanted to make my vision for the store a reality.

Excited, I grabbed a notebook I kept near the hallway door for capturing ideas and began jotting down notes. I'd filled half a page when I heard the bell out front jangle, signaling the arrival of a customer.

"I'll be right there," I called, hastily scribbling my thoughts before they skittered away like the last of autumn's leaves.

A jingling noise made me wonder if someone was playing with the bell, although it sounded different than usual. Annoyed, I shoved on the glasses I wore when there were customers in the store and rushed down the hallway, ready to admonish whoever was using the bell as a toy. Quite unexpectedly, I stepped out of the hallway, turned toward the door, and slammed into the broad chest of a man who smelled like leather, snowfall, and sunshine.

It was an entirely heady and altogether unwelcome combination. Almost as unwelcome as his hands on my arms, even if they did steady me and keep me upright.

With a jerk, I pulled out of his grasp, and stepped away. Expecting to see a face I knew, because it's a small town and that saying of everybody knows everyone is true, I saw a stranger. Not only was the man unknown to me, but I had to tip my head back to look up at a face covered with dark stubble and shadowed by the brim of a cowboy hat.

In the years I'd been away from Christmas Mountain, living in some of the biggest cities in the world, I'd learned to be careful, to stay on the defense for safety's sake. Some might go as far as to say I have an overly ambitious sense of stranger danger.

Everything about this brawny man put me on high alert. Warning bells clanged in my ears while my stomach cartwheeled with nerves. Normally, I don't have this type of reaction to my bookstore patrons. Or even people I've never met.

But something about this cowboy left me completely unsettled.

And I didn't like it. Not one bit.

I took another step back, my eyes fastened on his square-tipped fingers as they pushed back his hat. Involuntarily, a gasp rolled out of me at the sight of his handsome face. The notion that he could have stepped right out of the pages of a western clothing advertisement didn't seem far-fetched in the least. All he needed was a dusting of snow on his wide shoulders and a horse in the background.

Slightly disoriented by his rugged and undeniable masculinity, I took a moment to study his strong chin, wide mouth with lips any one of my friends would have labeled as sexy, and straight nose. Eyes the color of warm chocolate observed me with curiosity. Much to my dismay, my mouth began to water. I can't help it if I adore chocolate.

"Miss," he said, touching a finger to the brim of his hat. It was like watching a scene from one of my favorite John Wayne movies. "Could I please speak to the manager?"

What could this cowboy possibly need that required a conversation with the manager?

I shoved aside the desire to reach out and run my hand over his jaw. Instead, I yanked on my business owner persona. "I'm Carol Bennett, owner and manager of Rudolph's Reads." The hand I held out toward him remained unclaimed. His gaze raked over me from the messy bun on top of my head, across my unflattering glasses, over my long burgundy cardigan, loose cream dress, and black fur-flecked tights right down to my ballerina-style shoes that I'd picked up in Italy two years ago.

"Carol Burnett? Like the red-headed comedian?" He smiled, flashing white teeth, although the front two were slightly crooked. It was nice to know he was human with something flawed because up to that moment, he'd seemed too perfect to be real. "You know any song and dance routines?"

His hand engulfed mine as he shook it. The rough calluses on his palm created the strangest tingling sensation on my skin. It was almost like a static electricity shock, but far more electric and strangely exciting.

Distracted by my reaction to his touch, it took me a moment to realize he'd misheard my name. Although I was a Carol Burnett fan, I certainly didn't appreciate being teased by this man. Song and dance routine, indeed.

Insult and indignation warred within me as I tried not to glower at the dolt who'd worn spurs into my store. Good heavens! Would they scratch the hardwood floor? I certainly hoped not. A sudden urge to make him stand on the mat just inside the door nearly overcame me, but I tamped it down.

"Bennett, not Burnett. My name is Carol Bennett." I spoke loudly, slowly, and clearly, as though trying to communicate with a nearly deaf human who conversed in an entirely different language.

"Got it," he said, rocking back on one hip. The position drew my attention to his solid legs, thighs thick and straining against the denim of his jeans.

With a mental shake, I realized I was starting to think like a heroine in one of the western romance novels I liked to read. And that would never do, at least not where this man was concerned. I didn't know what it was about him that irked me so, but something did. There was something about this man that just made me want to shove him out the door.

And it couldn't all be blamed on the Carol

Burnett comment.

"Don't I know you?" He studied my face again. The intense perusal made me want to fidget or, at the very least, turn away and busy myself shelving books. In the back of the store. Far away from the good-looking cowboy.

Eyes locked on mine, he leaned toward me. "You sure look familiar."

Flashing red warning lights began blasting in my head. Time to deflect and distract.

I laughed, one of those insincere, fake laughs that always cue people that you're either wildly uncomfortable, nearly hysterical, or hiding something. In my case, it would have been all three.

With a shrug, I headed toward the island in the middle of the store. "I don't recall seeing you around town before. Did you recently move to Christmas Mountain or are you visiting someone in the area?"

"I live about fifteen miles out of town on a ranch with my grandmother. Been there since my grandpa passed away," he said, keeping step beside me. "Nana is quite a fan of Rudolph's Reads and sent me in to pick up some books she ordered. Truth be told, I'd rather be just about anywhere else." To emphasize his point, he glanced around like he might catch some horrible, highly contagious disease from the air in my store.

The red lights ceased flashing and I wracked my brain, trying to think who this man's grandmother might be. Certainly not one of my regular customers. Was there a cranky, wasp-tongued woman who'd recently ordered books that I couldn't remember? Maybe one of my employees waited on her while I was making a deposit at the bank or running errands.

"Her name?" I asked as I made my way behind the counter, ready to tap in a search on my computer.

"Nancy Wright."

Apparently, my jaw dropped open in shock because the man suddenly smirked and touched the bottom of my chin with the tip of his index finger, gently pushing upward. That simple touch sent an electric jolt through me that caused my mouth to snap shut with such force, my teeth rattled.

"You're lucky it's past fly season or you'd have a mouth full." His smirk grew even more annoying and cocky as he braced an elbow on the counter. "I reckon it's hard to believe my sweet nana could be related to me."

Feigning innocence, I reached beneath the counter and brought up the stack of books Nancy had ordered two weeks ago. Not only was she a great customer, but she was a wonderful woman who always brought a little sunshine to my life when she stopped by the store.

The last time she came in, she mentioned she planned to have hip replacement surgery and would be out of commission for a while. That's why she wanted the books. However, I had no idea the surgery would happen before the holidays.

"Did Nancy have surgery already? Is she doing well?" I asked, scanning the barcodes on the books and ringing up the total on the cash register.

"Nana is doing fine. I brought her home from

the hospital yesterday. I hadn't even finished breakfast this morning before she started hounding me about coming into town to get her books. It's a good thing I needed to run by the feed store anyway, so it isn't a wasted trip. It's a shame to come into town for no reason."

The fact his sweet grandmother wanted her books to read while she recuperated should have been plenty of reason for him to make a trip into Christmas Mountain. Did this man have any idea how utterly stupid and barbaric he sounded? A sudden vision of him roping some unfortunate woman and dragging her off like a primitive cavedweller made me work to subdue my smile as he paid for the books.

I accepted the cash the cowboy handed to me and made change. Hardly anyone paid with cash these days. Regardless, I had the distinct idea Nancy's grandson was anything but typical.

Nancy had mentioned him on occasion, but I couldn't recall his name. Jim? Tom? Maybe I should have paid more attention when she spoke about him. If I had my facts straight, he'd served in the Army, done a tour or two overseas where he saw combat, and came to Christmas Mountain to help run the ranch when Nancy's beloved husband, Bill, passed away. From the scant information she'd shared, I had no idea he was close to my age. I'd envisioned him as nearing middle age, balding, maybe with a beer belly.

Boy, was I wrong.

With all the well-meaning friends and customers who'd tried to set me up on dates in the past year, I'm surprised Nancy hadn't nudged me in that direction with her grandson. Had she told me he was incredibly handsome with enough swagger to make women swoon I wouldn't have accepted it as true. Some things had to be witnessed in person to believe.

I handed the bag of books to the man. When I did, our fingers brushed and it felt as though a charged jolt raced up my arm. It completely threatened to short circuit not only my stranger-danger vibe, but all my functioning brain cells.

It was just my luck to find myself attracted to someone I didn't particularly like. Honestly, I held no interest in pursuing a relationship with anyone right now, but especially not a cocky, too-handsome-for-his-own-good cowboy who kept staring at me in a way that made me feel vulnerable and exposed.

Which is why I wondered what alien had overtaken my body when I delayed his departure.

"I didn't catch your name," I blurted as he headed toward the door, spurs jangling in an admittedly pleasant way. I noted they weren't touching the floor and fears of damaged hardwood receded.

With quick steps, I hurried around the counter, uncertain why I didn't just let him leave and hope to goodness I'd never see him again.

He stopped and turned back to me. "Burke. Tim Burke."

An unexpected vision of the big man toppling into the snow, like a falling tree, struck me as ridiculously funny. Unable to stop myself, I snorted with laughter.

"Mind sharing the joke?" he asked in a frigid tone that would have turned water into ice in less than two seconds.

"Actually, I do," I said, struggling to curtail my humor at his expense.

Tim sighed in disgust. "Tim Burke… timber. You made the connection and found yourself quite amusing."

He strode over until he stood so close, I could see flecks of gold floating in the brown of his eyes and a mole by his right ear. Heat rolled off him and threatened to consume me. Slowly, I backed away from him until I bumped into the counter.

A disgruntled sigh rolled out of him as he frowned. "You aren't the first one to think of that and you won't be the last."

"I could say the same thing to you. Do you think you're the only one to make the Carol Burnett joke?" I shot back, standing as straight as I could stretch my spine. How tall was this guy, anyway? He stood a good five or six inches above me, and that rarely happened. The fact he was built like a lumberjack renewed my mirth about his name. Lest I break into another round of laughter, I bit my lip and glanced away.

I heard what could have been a derisive grunt as his spurs jingled, drawing my gaze back to him. He scowled at me and waggled a finger toward my head.

"No one would mistake you for Carol Burnett, even a younger version of her. You'd need a sense of humor and red hair." At the mention of hair, he stared at my face in a most disconcerting manner.

Since my back was pressed against the counter, I had no place to escape him when he took a step closer. As I breathed in his masculine, decadent scent, I wasn't sure I wanted to.

Fear of another human in my personal space overrode interest and I gave him a mighty shove that should have sent him stumbling backward. It didn't cause him to waver even a centimeter. Finally, he stepped back with a frustrated expression on his face. Then he trailed two steps behind me as I rushed over to the romance section and began straightening books that were already perfectly aligned on the shelves.

I could feel his presence directly beside me as I moved from romance to fuss with the items I'd already placed in the Christmas display.

"You are one prickly, jumpy, frosty woman. Do you assume all men are going to assault you or is it just me you so clearly don't like or trust? If I had to make a guess, I'd say you went out into the big, wide world and found you weren't the prettiest, smartest, most talented or adored female out there so you ran off with your tail between your legs. Nana said you grew up here. Guess Christmas Mountain makes a good place to hide from your failures."

Livid that he was partially right in his unwarranted assessment, I felt fury boil from my toes upward until my body vibrated with anger. My index finger poked into the canvas of the coat covering that granite-hard chest.

"Let me tell you something, Mr. Burke. You

don't know me, don't know anything about me, where I've been, or what I've been through. I'll thank you to keep your comments to yourself. Besides, you are the most outspoken, opinionated, obnoxious man I've had the misfortune of meeting in a long while, and that is truly saying something."

With each poke of my finger, he backed another step toward the door.

"Is that so?" he questioned when he stood on the mat in front of the door. The way he looked at me made me feel like he could see all the way down to my soul. It was unnerving.

His hand reached for the doorknob as he shot me a knowing glance. "You hide here at the bookstore because you're afraid of life, Miss Bennett. You hide behind your books, and your counter, with your messy hair, and clothes that would fit a woman four sizes bigger than you, not to mention those ridiculous glasses. I bet they aren't even prescription glasses." He shook his head, appearing disappointed. "Anyone with eyes in their head can see you're beautiful, no matter how hard you work to conceal it. You better be careful or you'll turn into one of those crazy old women whose only friends are the characters in the books she reads and the fourteen cats living in her apartment."

"I don't have fourteen cats!" I shouted, which drew Hemi from wherever he'd been hiding. For good measure, the feline meowed then rubbed against Tim's leg, purring enthusiastically. Normally, Hemi ignored most people, felt threatened by strangers, and preferred to stay in the storage room. Yet, here he was making friends with a man I'd quickly come to consider an enemy.

"Traitor," I whispered to the cat.

Before I could pick him up, Tim scooped him into one big hand, gave the cat a few scratches that earned Hemi's undying loyalty, and handed him to me.

"Thanks for Nana's books, Miss *Burnett*." Tim emphasized the use of the wrong last name. I knew because of the devilish smile he wore when he opened the door.

"You're welcome, Timber." I followed him outside, still holding the cat. "Don't fall off any stumps out there. Watch out for swinging axes!" I knew I sounded deranged as I stood on the sidewalk, yelling after him as he walked down the street. "And tell your grandmother I hope she's healing well."

He lifted a hand in the air, although I wasn't sure if it was to dismiss me or acknowledge he'd heard my comments.

"Argh!" Infuriated, exasperated, and more invigorated than I'd ever felt in my life, I returned inside and slammed the door. If I lived to be ninety, I hoped I never saw handsome, hunky Tim Burke again.

Yet, despite all the snarky, barbed comments we'd tossed at each other during our brief conversation, the idea he thought I was beautiful played over and over in my head.

## *Chapter Two*

"Just one more string of lights," I said to Aiden, Josie, and the friends they'd brought along to help turn my bookstore into a winter wonderland. Or maybe it was Christmas central.

At any rate, I was certain Santa would approve.

After my encounter with Tim Burke that morning, I'd been so energized, I could hardly stand still. In between helping customers, I ditched my original decorating ideas and came up with a new plan. One that would add an undeniable "Wow!" factor to my store.

By the time the kids arrived that afternoon, I'd already scoured the storage room and basement for any decorations and props we could use. A shot of excitement burst through me when I discovered two half-circle display shelves that graduated from wide at the bottom to narrow at the top. If I shoved them back-to-back, I was sure they could be used as a Christmas tree. Aiden and one of his friends carried them up from the basement while I sent Josie to the hardware store for paint. When they finished giving the shelves a new coat of paint, they sported a rich evergreen hue.

As we waited for the paint to dry, we created a window display with books and an animated elf that climbed up a ladder. Josie came up with the idea to prop the ladder against a tall stack of books then we added fake snow and lights to the window along with a miniature tree and tiny wrapped packages.

While the teens strung lights and draped garlands, I dug dusty silk poinsettias out of plastic storage tubs and cleaned them, setting them into pots wrapped with green foil and adorned with red and green plaid bows.

All of the students stayed past closing time to help finish the displays, so I ordered pizza and had it delivered. They laughed and teased while they ate, reminding me of fun times I'd spent with my friends during our high school years.

Once the last piece of pizza had been consumed, we turned our attention to the display shelves we set up at the back of the Christmas section. The kids ran around the store, gathering every holiday-themed book they could find then we set them on the shelves. Josie and the girls added small gift items tucked among the books while the boys figured out how to attach a large crystal star to the top of the display. We draped white lights along the shelves then stepped back to survey our handiwork.

"It's beautiful," Josie said, a look of awe on her face.

"It looks really good," Aiden said, grinning at me. "What else can we do?"

I laughed and motioned toward the door. "Go home. You all have done far more than I dreamed we'd accomplish this evening. It's late and I'm sure your folks will be wondering where you are."

The kids gathered their coats and backpacks. Before they could leave, I paid Aiden's and Josie's friends for their time.

"You don't have to pay us, Miss Bennett," one of the boys said, trying to hand back the envelope I'd given him.

"Yeah. It was cool to get to help." Another boy held out his envelope. "Besides, you fed us pizza."

I shook my head. "You earned every penny of that. Truly, I appreciate the help. Now, get out of here."

Aiden pulled open the door and held it as the teens hurried out into the cold. "It was fun, Carol. See you tomorrow."

"I can't thank you and Josie enough for bringing reinforcements. I'll include a little gratitude in your next paycheck."

Aiden's grin widened and Josie gave me a hug before they raced after their friends.

I locked the door and made sure the open sign was turned to closed then surveyed the store. To get the full effect of the decorations, I turned off the lights and admired the Christmas lights twinkling among the books and along the ceiling.

A squeal of excitement might have escaped before I could hold it back. Who am I kidding? I was so giddy, I probably looked like a hyped-on-sugar six-year-old as I danced around the store, singing "Holly, Jolly Christmas" at the top of my lungs.

Hemi wandered out from his bed in the storage room to see what all the racket was about, took one look at me, and made his way upstairs, ready to go to the apartment. With one more glance at my store, and exuberant over how festive it appeared, I unplugged the lights and went upstairs.

The next morning, I bounced out of bed at five, eager to begin the day. I dressed in my workout clothes and made my way downstairs to the area in the basement where I'd set up a home gym. I hopped on the treadmill and ran four miles before I settled onto a mat on the floor and got in some much-needed stretches. I rolled from one side to the other only to discover a pair of eyeballs so close to mine, I could count individual eyelashes.

Startled, I jerked back while Hemi glared at me like I'd offended him. The cat rarely entered the basement and never came downstairs while I was exercising, so I don't know what inspired him to do so this morning. I gave him a few scratches then went back to stretching. Only Hemi had other ideas. Every time I moved, I either had his tail or a paw in my face. After five minutes of trying to get him to stop, I gave up and held him on my lap while he purred in bliss.

"You are the strangest cat, Hemi. Do you know

that?"

More purrs provided his response to my question.

Aware I wasn't getting in any more exercise with Hemi's unwanted assistance, I carried him upstairs to the storage room then opened the back door, letting him out for a few minutes. I left the door open a crack and the chilly air made the sweat on my skin feel as though it might turn to ice. Quickly filling his food and water bowls, I stepped to the far side of the room, away from the door, waiting for the cat. He pranced in and headed straight for his breakfast.

I shut the door and locked it, rubbing my hands on my bare arms to warm my skin as I rushed upstairs to my apartment. At least I could get ready this morning without him sitting outside the bathroom door, yowling at me to hurry things along.

After indulging in a long, hot shower, I blow-dried my hair and stared at the reflection in the mirror, something I hadn't done in more than a year.

Natural golden highlights accent my thick, light brown hair. They don't look like much indoors, but out in the sun, they shine. My eyes are blue, the color of cornflowers, if my dad's description could be believed. And I'm fortunate to have long eyelashes that curl slightly on the ends. My cheekbones are prominent, but my skin is clear and smooth with peachy undertones. Thanks to two years of braces, I had straight, white teeth and a mouth that wasn't too wide or too small. If asked, my mother would say my chin is stubborn, but since we weren't speaking, I guess I can describe it any way I like.

Someone had once told me my face was symmetrical perfection. Of course, they wanted something from me, so the flattery was most likely fake. Men had commented on my delicate facial structure, some had told me I was beautiful, and others had leered at me until I wanted to run away. My looks had been what drove me away from Christmas Mountain and the very reason I'd returned.

Thoughts of what had happened during the years I'd been gone made me edgy, so I tucked them back inside the box at the back of my mind, slammed the mental lid, and dressed for the day. As I slipped on an oversized blouse, Tim Burke's comment about wearing clothes that would fit a woman four sizes bigger taunted me. He wasn't wrong.

When you want to avoid people seeing you a certain way, you have to guide them a different direction, which is why I generally wore loose blouses or dresses with sweaters or vests. Camouflaging my shape had morphed into an art I'd perfected. I picked up the glasses I wore in the store and considered how Tim knew I didn't need to wear them. The lenses were clear with no prescription. They were just one more piece of what I viewed as a disguise.

Did other people know? I hoped not.

Of all the people in Christmas Mountain, the only one who knew the full truth about me, about my past, was Mr. Abernathy, and he'd take my secrets to his grave. Ms. King knew, but she was gone now. Only a few other people knew all about my past, but I trusted them with my life and they'd never set foot in Christmas Mountain, anyway.

Bothered by my morning musings, I made a cup of pumpkin spice tea and toasted a bagel, savoring the simple meal in my favorite chair. Hemi wandered into the apartment, since I'd left the door open for him, and plopped down on my foot. He rolled from his back to his side a few times, before curling up and closing his eyes. Apparently, tormenting me while I attempted to exercise was exhausting.

With a smile at the crazy cat, I picked up a book I'd started reading a few days ago and managed to read through a page or two before ponderings about Tim infiltrated my thoughts and left me unable to concentrate.

The man was built like a tree, sturdy and solid. From bumping into him, I could tell there were muscles aplenty beneath his coat and shirt. Long, strong legs, that kissable mouth, and eyes that looked like melted chocolate would captivate any woman.

When I started imagining what it would feel like to have him hold me in his arms against that broad chest, I hopped up and scurried into the kitchen. I made a second cup of tea, gathered my things, and headed toward the door.

"Hemi, let's go. I've got things to do downstairs."

From my position near the door, I watched as the cat lazily stretched, as though he needed time to consider if he'd get up or go back to sleep.

"Hemi, move it," I said. The stern tone of my voice got him up and sauntering toward the door. He paused long enough to stop and rub against my leg, leaving a wide path of cat hair on my dark blue leggings.

Involuntarily, my eyes rolled upward as I followed Hemi out of the apartment and shut the door.

He scampered downstairs and disappeared into the storage room while I turned on equipment, flicked on light switches, then plugged in the strands of Christmas lights. The twinkle of hundreds of little lights lightened my mood and made me smile.

The day passed quickly and before I knew it, Aiden swept the floor and gathered the trash while I took care of the day's bookwork and prepared the bank deposit.

He was almost to the door when he glanced back at me. "Are you doing anything special tomorrow for Thanksgiving?"

I nodded my head. "Yes, I've got plans. Are your folks still planning to host all your family?" I asked as I stepped around the counter and over to the door.

"Unfortunately, yes. My sisters are home from college, my grandparents are coming from Great Falls, and my aunt Tracey will be there with her horrible kids. The last time they came, my cousins destroyed everything." Aiden looked like he anticipated the visit with all the delight one would use to welcome a herd of stampeding elephants.

"It's going to be awful."

I patted him on the back. "I'm sure it won't be that bad. Try to enjoy the day, Aiden, and have a happy Thanksgiving."

"I'll try." He opened the door and stepped outside. "Thanks for scheduling me to work Friday. It gives me a great reason to escape my family."

I laughed and gave him a nudge forward. "Get out of here."

He grinned and jogged down the street. He only lived a few blocks from the store so it wouldn't take him long to reach the warmth of home. When I hired him, he told me he wanted to earn money to buy a car so he could have transportation to get himself out of Christmas Mountain the moment he graduated from high school. Since he was a junior, I wondered if he'd change his mind before then.

Often, he talked about the places he wanted to visit and the things he wanted to see. He mentioned backpacking across Europe with a group of friends more than once. I could have told him some great places to visit if he did it, but kept my mouth shut. The less people knew about me and where I'd spent my time since graduating and leaving town, the better.

In ways, Aiden reminded me of my younger self. I was just as hungry for adventure, just as eager to experience life as he was. And I did follow my dreams for a while. Then I got a big, fat reality check.

One that still left me reeling.

Hemi wandered into the store and meowed as he made his way around the displays over to the stairs.

"I'm ready to head up, too, Hemi." I quickly locked the door, turned off the lights, and rushed upstairs.

I ate a salad and perused the viewing selections on TV, disgusted to realize my thoughts had once again turned to Tim Burke.

"Stop being an idiot," I muttered, earning an odd glimpse from the cat.

As much as I disliked Nancy's grandson, I had no idea why I couldn't seem to get him and those warm chocolate brown eyes of his out of my head.

Thankfully, before I could give him more thought, the phone rang. I glanced at the caller ID, surprised to see a New York number.

"Hello," I answered cautiously.

"Hey, girl! Happy almost Thanksgiving. How are things in the sticks?"

I grinned, glad to hear from my friend, Lacey Lane. She worked as a publicist on a reality TV show in New York. We met when I first landed in the city after leaving Christmas Mountain. We clicked and had been good friends since then. I knew Lacey had been busy filming a new dating show, at least she was when I spoke to her a month ago.

"Happy almost Thanksgiving, Lacey. What are you doing up so late?" I asked, then realized late for Montana would be barely winding down time in New York.

"Late?" she asked, sounding surprised. "Isn't it like eight there? You truly are embracing your roots, aren't you?"

Before I could reply, she laughed. "Don't you remember the time we stayed out until four in the morning with those two guys who…"

The last thing I needed was a trip down memory lane with Lacey. "That was forever ago. I'd like to think we've grown up and matured since then."

"I suppose we have," Lacey conceded. "But we did have a lot of fun. Then you had to go and get yourself into this mess that left you cowering in the shadows in Hickville."

I sighed. "Christmas Mountain is not Hickville. It's a perfectly lovely little town in the mountains. In fact, you should come for a visit sometime. I think you'd love it." I could just picture Lacey strolling down Main Street in one of her chic outfits, surveying the town with a critical eye and a dash of her ever-present humor.

"Maybe I'll come for a visit next year. Things are really busy with work right now."

"What's going on?" I settled back into the soft cushions of my couch and enjoyed a good chat with Lacey.

She told me about a guy she'd been dating who'd turned out to be another dud.

"What about you? Any tall, dark and handsome cowboys sweeping you off your feet?" Lacey asked. "Any good-looking guys catching your eye?"

"No!" I nearly shouted.

"Spill right now, Carol Bennett! You have met somebody. The way you said no sounds more like a 'oh, yeah!' to me. Who is he? What's his name? What does he do?"

Rats. Of course, Lacey would pick up my too quick denial that there was no one of interest in Christmas Mountain. In truth, I'd hardly been able to get Tim Burke out of my head long enough to function since he'd strolled out of my store with those spurs jingling like Christmas bells.

"There isn't anyone, not like you think, Lace. This obnoxious, know-it-all cowboy came into the store yesterday to pick up his grandmother's books and he was absolutely infuriating!"

"Was he tall? Taller than you?"

"Yes, but what's that got to do with anything?"

"Everything. How about handsome? What does he look like?"

I envisioned Tim's sensuous mouth, his warm brown eyes, the strong jaw covered in rakish stubble. "Homely. So homely."

Lacey laughed. "I bet he's one of those men so rugged and virile, he looks like he belongs on a magazine cover."

Maybe, but I sure wasn't going to tell her that.

"I need to run, Carol. I'm supposed to meet someone in ten minutes and if I don't hurry, I'll be late."

"Got a hot date?" I asked, wishing Lacey could find someone who made her feel like a queen instead of dating guys who ended up turning into frogs.

"Don't I wish. No, it's a work thing."

I could hear the jangle of keys and imagined her gathering her things from her office and speeding out the door. "I'm glad you called, Lacey. It's always nice to connect with you. Take care and have a wonderful Thanksgiving."

"I will. Just promise me you won't sit alone in your apartment, hiding away from the world. Call that infuriating cowboy and see if he'd like to help you stuff a turkey."

Since I had no intention of ever speaking to Tim again, I feigned a bad connection. "I'm losing reception. Talk to you soon!"

## *Chapter Three*

Although I'd told Aiden I had special plans for Thanksgiving, the truth was I had nothing going on.

My so-called plans included sleeping in, eating a frozen turkey dinner, and reading or watching movies.

I could have accepted the invitations offered by friends to join them for dinner, but I politely refused. It's weird being at a gathering of family members on a holiday, especially when you aren't family. And with my current situation, it makes for a nerve-wracking experience. I much prefer a quiet day alone, or at least I convinced myself of that.

Years have passed since I celebrated any holiday with my family. I never met my grandparents, was an only child, and have no idea if aunts, uncles, or cousins exist. My dad died from an aneurysm two months before my high school graduation. My mother and I have never been close. We've only spoken twice in the last nine years. Last I heard, she'd moved to California and married a plastic surgeon. Maybe he could make her appear as perfect as she always expected me to look.

With my thoughts about to spiral in a depressing direction, I snatched them back on track and stretched lazily in bed.

It was almost eight. Rare were the days when I slept past six. With nothing else to do, I was in no hurry to climb from beneath the warm covers.

However, someone failed to give Hemi that memo as he stood next to the bed, glowering at me. When I'd first taken him in, I made it clear he was welcome anywhere in my apartment, except on my bed. The thought of waking up with his face or, horror of all horrors, tail in my face was enough to keep me from allowing him to snuggle on the bed.

He made up for that slight by loudly demanding I get up. Right now. Although I'd left a dish of dry cat food for him in the kitchen, he was particular about where he ate.

"Fine, I'm up," I said, rolling out of bed and shoving my feet into a pair of fuzzy slippers that looked like a bright pink monster attempted to consume me, toes first. I snagged a thick robe I'd purchased in Spain that was so soft and warm it felt like being wrapped in clouds on a summer day.

Hemi stood at the apartment door, tail swishing impatiently as I rammed my arms into the sleeves of the robe and tied the belt around my waist. The moment I opened the door, he scurried around the bookcase, down the stairs, and toward the storage room. I yawned as I made my way there, opening the door so he could race outside. I filled his food bowl, gave him fresh water, and was glad I'd remembered to clean his litter box last night so I wouldn't have to deal with it today.

He wasn't outside long before he raced back in and over to his food bowl· where he started crunching his food like he hadn't eaten in weeks.

"You have a flair for drama, Hemi." Then again, so did his namesake.

I shuffled back upstairs, made a cup of cranberry tea, and sipped it while watching the Macy's Thanksgiving Day Parade. Bored by the time I'd sat through thirty minutes of it, I decided to go for a walk. No one would pay any attention to me and I could use the fresh air to clear my mind which seemed to be tripping all over itself today.

I started to pull on sweats then changed my mind. In the mood to dress more like I used to, I tossed the sweats in a drawer. After a quick shower, I slid into a pair of designer jeans and a chunky cream sweater I'd picked up in Ireland. Although I rarely wear makeup anymore or do anything with my hair other than twist it into a bun, I added a touch of mascara, a swipe of lip gloss, and spent twenty minutes curling my hair. The odds of me running into anyone were slim to none. All my friends would be busy getting ready for a big turkey dinner. But it felt good to spend a little time on my appearance today.

Ready to go, I pulled on a pair of brown leather boots I'd purchased in Morocco then grabbed my coat, scarf, and a pair of gloves.

Quickly gathering my keys, wallet, and phone, I tucked them into my pockets and hurried downstairs. Rather than go out the back and walk through the alley, I unlocked the front door, stepped outside, and locked it again.

The air was crisp and fallen leaves skittered down the sidewalk as I strolled away from my shop. With no destination in mind, I meandered along Main Street, glancing in the quaint shop windows. I loved that the buildings were brick, most of them tall and narrow. It gave the street such a tidy, inviting appearance.

I walked past the Sleigh Café and the grocery store where Jingle Bells Bakery was located. They sold some of the best cinnamon rolls I've ever tasted. Realizing I was hungry, I should have eaten breakfast or at least grabbed a bagel or granola bar before I left for my jaunt.

For a moment, I considered walking over to The Falls, a waterfall that was near the center of town, but instead wandered along the nearly empty streets.

The fourth time my stomach growled, I changed direction and headed back toward my shop. I unlocked the door and barely stepped inside before Hemi zoomed up to me, as though I'd left him alone for months instead of less than an hour.

"What has gotten into you lately?" I asked the cat as I picked him up and carried him with me to the apartment. I toasted an English muffin and topped it with cream cheese and chocolate spread before taking a bite. I eat healthy ninety-percent of the time, so occasional indulgences are acceptable. The other day, an individual-sized chocolate cake beckoned to me from the bakery. I bought it to enjoy with a pint of caramel cone ice cream, my favorite, after my microwavable turkey dinner.

I made a cup of maple apple tea and sank onto the sofa. Hemi curled up beside me and went to sleep.

As I ate my bagel, I turned on the television and found a second airing of the parade. Apparently, the stroll had calmed my anxiety because I settled back and viewed the floats, bands, and huge balloons on the TV with a smile.

The longer I watched, the more I relaxed. My eyelids grew heavy and I was almost asleep when I heard what sounded like the bell jingle downstairs. That was impossible. The store was closed. The door was locked. Besides, no one in their right mind would want to be at the bookstore today. Not when there were family meals waiting to be consumed. I could almost taste the creamy mashed potatoes and smell the spices in a homemade pumpkin pie I imagined would be served at homes throughout Christmas Mountain.

Convinced I was hearing things, I returned to watching TV. Everything was fine until I heard the stairs creak a few minutes later.

Freaked out that someone was in the store, I jumped up and glanced around. I had a baseball bat in my bedroom closet, but wasn't sure I could actually bring myself to hit someone with it. The creaking on the stairs grew louder and my panic escalated. At least the old steps prevented anyone from sneaking up them.

As quietly as I could, I crept over to my open apartment door and tiptoed over to the bookcase. I'd left the panel open so Hemi could come and go as he pleased throughout the day. Now, I wished I'd pushed it shut when I returned from my walk.

Footsteps sounded on the landing then stopped. If someone planned on robbing the place, they'd be downstairs breaking into the cash register, not skulking around on the stairs. Was someone looking for me specifically, or just casing the joint?

Obviously, I'd watched one too many detective shows. I closed my eyes, took a deep breath, and thought of all the self defense and martial arts classes I'd taken. When you live on your own in a big city, it's a handy thing to know how to protect yourself. I'd even earned a brown belt in karate before I had to drop out of my class.

Whoever was on the other side of the bookcase was most likely not aware of my skills, which gave me an advantage and a dose of courage.

With another deep breath, I rushed around the bookcase and went into full-on attack-ninja mode. My hand was less than an inch away from chopping into the intruder's windpipe when I realized the man was calling me by name.

"Carol! Hold on! It's okay!" The voice didn't sound scared, but slightly pained.

I stopped before I did more damage, pushed my hair out of my eyes, and glared at Tim Burke. The shocked look on his face was enough to make me feel a slight twinge of remorse for striking first and asking questions later.

"What are you doing here?" I asked in a terse tone, dropping my hands and stepping back.

It took him a moment to respond. He bent over and retrieved the hat I'd knocked off his head to the floor. It gave me the opportunity to note he had dark brown hair, worn in a crew cut that somehow suited him. It also let me observe his backside in snug-fitting jeans. The sight was enough to make my eyes widen in acute appreciation. The guy must have a girlfriend or wife. Incredibly good-looking men typically didn't stay unattached for long.

Once he'd picked up his hat and brushed it off, he held it in his right hand while his left rubbed over his jaw. There was a distinct possibility I hit it with my fist, or possibly a foot. Then again, it might have been when he dodged away from me and collided with a sconce on the wall.

He worked his jaw from side to side before he sighed and looked at me again. It was then I noticed a scratch on his cheek with a drop of blood about to drip from it.

Remorse settled over me. Even if he had no business in my store, I didn't mean to hurt him. If he was there for nefarious reasons, he would have likely done something by now instead of glaring at me like I'd lost my mind.

"Come on," I said and tipped my head toward my apartment then walked around the end of the bookcase. I didn't look back to see if he followed, but the sound of his boots on the hardwood let me know he was right behind me.

I led the way to my kitchen where I ripped a paper towel off the roll, dampened it, then dabbed at his cheek.

Rather than apologize, I repeated my earlier question, minus the attitude. "What are you doing here?"

"Nana made me come. She's convinced you are spending the day alone and rambled on about you most likely eating a frozen dinner and having no one but your cat to talk to," Tim said looking at my ceiling as I continued to press the paper towel to his cheek. "I didn't break in, if that's what you're thinking. The door was unlocked. I looked around downstairs, but didn't see you. Nana mentioned you live above the store, so I came upstairs."

"You should have yelled for me." Or worn his jangly spurs. That would have been a good giveaway a cowboy had entered my domain uninvited.

"I didn't want to startle you."

I couldn't stop from smirking. "How'd that work out for you?"

He rubbed his jaw where the skin was already bruising. "Not well."

"You know, they have this thing called a telephone," I said, unable to reel in the sarcasm. "Most people call if they have a question rather than drive fifteen miles into town for no reason. You can't pick up a load of feed today because I know for a fact the store's closed."

He grinned, then grimaced at the pain it must have caused. "I told Nana to call you, but she wouldn't calm down until I agreed to come get you. If you want to be mad at someone, take it up with her."

I stopped dabbing at his cheek and studied the cut. "It was kind of her to think of me, but I'll pass on the invitation."

"You have other plans?" Tim asked, looking down at me with a knowing expression on his face.

What clued him in to my pathetic holiday? The parade blaring on the TV or the little chocolate cake on the counter, still in its serving-for-one plastic container.

"Of sorts," I said, unwilling to outright lie.

He leaned back and studied me for a moment. "You look… different. Have a hot date?"

Did Hemi and a John Wayne marathon count?

"Are you okay?" I asked, not answering his question. I hadn't gone on a date in so long, hot or otherwise, I wasn't sure I even remembered how the whole dating thing worked.

"I'm fine," he said, straightening to his full height although I saw him wince and tuck his arm against his side.

"Let me at least get some peroxide for your cheek." I didn't wait for him to argue as I left the kitchen and hurried into my bathroom. I returned to find him in the living room on the couch with Hemi on his lap. The cat looked like he'd found his long-lost best friend.

Furry turncoat.

When I pressed a cotton ball soaked in peroxide against Tim's cheek, he squirmed like I attempted to pour flesh-eating acid over his skin.

"Are you five or a grown up?" I asked as he continued turning his face away from my hand.

"It depends on the day," he said in a deep voice

that seemed to rumble through my whole apartment. His hand caught my wrist and held it away from him.

I checked to make sure he wasn't attempting to electrocute me since something charged raced up my arm and out to every extremity.

Abruptly he released my hand and went back to scratching Hemi's back. The cat's purrs increased in volume. "What's his name?"

"Hemi." I dropped the cotton ball in the trash then observed as the cowboy pet my cat. He looked far too at home and comfortable in my apartment. And I hated to admit it, but I liked seeing him there. Hemi was quite discerning when it came to humans, besides me. The fact he cozied right up to Tim made me think he was probably a good guy under his opinionated, outspoken exterior.

"Like the engine?" he asked

I couldn't stop my eyes from rolling. "It doesn't surprise me in the least a guy like you would automatically jump to that conclusion. He is not named after car parts. He's named after Hemingway. Perhaps you've heard of him. He wrote books."

He didn't even lift his eyes from the cat as he continued petting him. "I have heard of Hemingway." He glanced up at me and spouted, "'The best way to find out if you can trust somebody is to trust them.'"

Point taken, and bonus points to the cowboy for not only knowing a Hemingway quote, but reciting one so particularly appropriate for the situation.

Other than aggravating me beyond endurance

the other day, he really hadn't done anything to make me think he had evil motives.

As I studied him with Hemi, watched those long fingers run through the cat's fur, any number of ideas, all of them unsettling, raced through my head. Before I did something insane, like sit beside Tim and rest my head against his brawny shoulder, I needed him to leave. Veiled insults hadn't worked, so perhaps I needed to take a direct approach.

"I really do appreciate Nancy's invitation and you driving all the way here to extend it, but I can't make it today."

There. That should make it clear I had no interest in going to the ranch.

"Nana said you'd say that and to tell you she won't accept no as an answer. Unless you want me to bodily pack you out to my pickup, you should get your things so we can go. My aunt Charli came to stay until Nana is back on her feet and she's a retired chef. She worked in Chicago at some fancy places. You ever hear of Magdala? She was the head chef there for ten years. I promise the food will be worth the trip."

Now he was playing dirty. Not only had I heard of Magdala, but I'd eaten there a few times. The food was out-of-this-world delicious.

I never learned to cook and my mother was not exactly Harriet homemaker during my growing up years. The thought of a home-cooked meal, made by a talented chef, was enough incentive to get me to go with Tim, no matter how much I wanted to pretend I wasn't interested.

"I don't want to intrude on your family

gathering," I said, still scrambling for excuses even as I thought about what I had on hand I could take as a hostess gift.

Tim scoffed. "Our family gathering consists of me, Aunt Charli, and Nana, and maybe one or two of the hired hands who don't have better offers."

"Oh, well, I…"

He set Hemi on the couch and stood. "Just agree to come. If you don't, Nana will never let me hear the end of it." Those big hands settled on my arms. A jolt rocked through me at his touch and I hoped he didn't notice my legs trembling from the contact.

When I continued to hesitate, he bent his knees and fused his gaze to mine. "Please?"

Warm chocolate eyes were evidently my kryptonite, because I nodded my head in agreement.

He grinned and dropped his hands. "Anything you need to do before we go?" he asked, looking around my apartment. I wondered what he saw as he studied my eclectic mix of furniture and decor. There were antiques I'd picked up here and there, a few things from my many travels abroad, and more modern pieces, like the comfy couch and big screen television.

"I'll just grab a few things and be ready to go." I rushed into the kitchen, snagged an empty basket from the pantry and filled it with an assortment of tea, something I always had plenty of on hand. I added a box of expensive chocolates I also liked to keep readily available. I usually ordered half a dozen boxes at a time and kept them in the freezer. I'd gotten this one out a few days ago thinking about enjoying a piece, or five, this weekend. I figured if I survived Black Friday, I deserved a treat.

I carried the basket into the living room where Tim waited with Hemi. When I picked up my coat, Tim hurried to hold it for me. Nice manners, that was unexpected. Then again, Nancy was a delightful woman and I would have expected no less from her grandson, if I hadn't known her grandson was Tim. After our encounter the other day, I would have labeled him as boorish and too lunkheaded to ever behave like a gentleman. Apparently, I was wrong.

Quickly tucking my wallet, phone, and keys inside my purse, I rubbed a hand over Hemi's back. "You be a good boy while I'm gone. No hairballs, gifts of rodents, or other similar surprises."

The cat swished his tail then licked his foot, as though he didn't care if I stayed or left.

"Fickle feline," I murmured as I walked over to my apartment door. Tim lifted his hat from where he'd left it on my pie crust table and followed me downstairs. I detoured over to the section of cozy mysteries Nancy preferred, and picked up one I knew she didn't have. I jotted a quick note and left it on my desk so I wouldn't forget to remove it from inventory, then walked out the front door. I double-checked to make sure it was locked before I turned around. Tim stood at the open passenger door of a big, black, double cab pickup. There weren't any running boards, but with my long legs I didn't need them.

He started to give me a hand, but I hopped in

before he could touch me. The look he gave me was one I couldn't decipher, so I didn't even try. I buckled my seatbelt while he jogged around to the driver's side and got behind the wheel.

As he backed out of the parking space in front of my store, I wondered what I had done. I'd never even checked to verify Nancy really was his grandmother. What if he was an imposter? Someone trying to get me off alone to...

Covertly as I could, I studied him. He was still as handsome as he'd been the other day, maybe even more so. Well, he would have been except for the cut on his cheek and a rapidly-forming bruise on his jaw. I should have filled a bag of ice for him to put on his jaw.

It's possible I might have gotten a teensy bit carried away in my self-defense moves. Then again, he could have at least called out my name before he started up the stairs. If he had, the martial arts exhibition could have been avoided.

Silence lingered between us as he drove out of town heading south toward Kalispell. I stared out the window at the beautiful landscape, thinking I really should get out more. Generally, I chose a Sunday afternoon every month or two and drove into Kalispell to stock up on supplies not readily available in Christmas Mountain. There was even a mall there where I could wander through clothing stores and sniff perfume and lotion samples (which I loved). And I'd eat at a favorite restaurant, then order extra to take home that would serve as my dinner for a few nights.

Nancy had mentioned Aspen Grove Ranch was

south of town, but that's about all I knew. We'd gone eight miles, by my calculations, from Christmas Mountain when Tim turned off the highway and headed west.

It took a good deal of effort on my part to maintain my calm façade. Inside, I was running a dozen scenarios through my mind of all the things that could happen to me. No one knew who I was with. Where I'd gone. Would anyone miss me if Tim turned out to be a perverted stalker or serial killer.

Then again, Hemi *had* given him a stamp of approval, so I was probably safe.

"You look nice." Tim's voice broke through my thoughts.

Taken aback that he'd offer me a compliment, I shifted my focus from the landscape to him. The shy, lopsided grin on his face appeared more sincere than any other expression I'd seen so far, except maybe the one of shock when I beat him up earlier. Okay, so I didn't beat him up, but I did get in a few serious licks.

Right now, I was much more interested in what he said than what had happened earlier. "Thank you."

He lifted his hand and waved it in my general direction. "You should dress like that more often instead of trying to look like Professor Trelawney from…"

"Harry Potter!" we said in unison, then he chuckled.

I didn't know whether to be amused or offended by the comparison, or just stunned that he made it in the first place. Even if he was closer to the truth than I cared to consider. Besides, I'd only seen him once the other day. How could he possibly know what I looked like the rest of the time?

Tim Burke seemed far too perceptive for my liking. He glanced at me again. "Nana mentioned you like to wear clothes that are…loose."

Now I wondered if he read minds. If that was even a remote possibility, I was in big trouble, considering the thoughts I was thinking earlier as I stared at his fine caboose when he bent over to pick up his hat.

"And you seem to like dressing like a cowboy." There, that should guide the conversation away from my attire.

Rather than the snarky retort I anticipated, he remained silent. A slow, tantalizing grin creased his cheeks and he looked like he tried to swallow back a laugh.

"What's funny?" I asked, assuming he'd thought of something amusing at my expense.

He glanced over at me then back at the road, still grinning. "I was just picturing the look on Miles' face if I walked into the feedstore and asked him for a pair of purple skinny jeans in my size."

A vision of Tim trying to squeeze his big, buff bod into a pair of tiny pants caused me to giggle.

Tim chuckled and looked my way again. "I think I better stick with what works."

No argument from me. What he had going on was definitely working. He smelled like horses, snow, and sunshine with something masculine and intriguing thrown in that made me want to draw in deep breaths of his scent. From the top of his cowboy hat to the tips of his boots, there was no mistaking the fact he was all rugged man and all cowboy.

Even his pickup shouted his chosen career path. Worn leather gloves, coils of rope, a set of hay tongs (don't ask how I know what those are), a smattering of hay leaves, and a saddle blanket in the back seat all attested to the fact this man knew a thing or two about rural life. If that wasn't enough, country music played softly on the radio.

It had been years since I'd listened to country music and I suddenly remembered how much I liked it. While I was away from Christmas Mountain, doing my best to pretend I was sophisticated and savvy in the ways of the world, I mostly listened to jazz or pop music. At the store, I played music that wasn't distracting to shoppers. But as I listened to an old Wade Hayes song about being old enough to know better and still too young to care, it made me smile.

I wondered if Tim was still too young to care. Somehow, I got the idea he was far past that stage of his life.

Unable to fully contain my tumbling thoughts, I gave him a quick glance. "So, Nancy mentioned you were in the Army. Was that something you did right out of high school?"

He nodded, but kept his gaze fastened on the road in front of him. "Yep."

I waited for him to elaborate, but evidently, he didn't feel inclined. But since I'd rather talk about him than me, I pressed ahead. "How long did you serve?"

"Eight years."

A two-word answer. I was making progress. "Where were you stationed?"

"Overseas." He looked over at me then back at the road. "Most of the time was in Afghanistan and Syria."

"Oh," I said, wishing I hadn't pushed him to answer. Clearly, he'd been in war zones. From the tightness of his jaw (the one that wasn't bruised) and the sound of his voice, I got the idea he preferred not to discuss this particular topic.

For a few minutes, neither of us said anything. Then Tim cleared his throat. "You did a good job decorating your store. It looks festive."

"Thank you." I offered him a smile, taking the olive branch he'd extended. "I have two high school students who work for me in the afternoons and they brought friends to help. Otherwise, I'd still be stringing lights and hanging garlands, trying to get ready for tomorrow."

"Tomorrow?" his forehead furrowed in a frown.

"Black Friday? You know, early morning shoppers full of caffeine and the need to find bargains." Did he ever leave the ranch? Visit a city? Listen to the news? How could you turn on the television and not notice the gazillion Black Friday ads that had been airing the past few weeks?

"What time will you open the bookstore?" he asked.

"At six. I have two employees who'll be there when we open and another who'll come at eight. I plan to close early tomorrow because honestly, no one is going to be out shopping after mid-afternoon and we'll all be worn out by then." I both dreaded and anticipated the biggest shopping day of the year. I hoped we did a record business, but I also wanted people to walk inside my store and feel happy to be there. I should have probably worked on sprucing up a few more displays or something along those lines today, but I needed a break. Going to Aspen Grove Ranch had definitely not been on my agenda, but now that we were almost there, I was glad I came.

"Nana mentioned you haven't had the store long. Did you own a store before you moved back to Christmas Mountain?"

"I've had the store about a year and no, I wasn't in retail before I moved back. But I worked at Rudolph's Reads when I was in high school and spent a lot of my childhood there, lost in the adventures of books."

He offered me a speculative glance. "You don't strike me as the book nerd type. I picture you more as a cheerleader or star of the class play, maybe a beauty contestant."

I blinked at him, unable to formulate words when he had so accurately described my high school years. Well, I wasn't a cheerleader, but I was in the class play and the beauty contestant thing was real. All too real.

"Hmm. I must have guessed at least one of those correctly. I picture you as a little shy, but nudged into doing things outside your comfort zone." He grinned. "How am I doing so far?"

Too well to suit me, but I won't tell him that. As far as me being nudged outside my comfort zone, it was more like shoved and pushed, or dragged unwillingly.

"I picture you as an athlete, probably football or wrestling," I said, envisioning a teen version of the burly man sitting on the other side of the pickup. "You probably had more friends than you could count, girls chasing you every time you turned around, and a devil-may-care attitude."

It was his turn to stare at me speechless. He finally looked back at the road and slowed down as we approached a turnoff with a metal Aspen Grove sign hanging in front of a pole fence. He turned onto the lane before he glanced back at me. "I think Nana has been talking about me way more than she should be."

"That wasn't from your grandmother. Nancy only said you'd been in the service and came to the ranch when your grandfather passed away. Other than that, she hasn't mentioned much about you." Which I still found so strange. Had the woman known Tim would rub me the wrong direction? If so, that would be a good reason she'd basically kept him a secret. I still have no idea how I lived in Christmas Mountain for a year and never ran into him before. Then again, I got the idea he only left the ranch when forced or for supplies.

I looked out the window in awe as he drove the pickup in front of a two-story log cabin home that looked like something out of a travel magazine. The porch that stretched across the front, complete with heavy pine rocking chairs, appeared so welcoming.

A few resilient mums still bloomed in flowerbeds along the front of the porch and a large yard surrounded the house, although the grass was now a shade of winter brown. In the distance, I could see cattle and horses with the backdrop of the mountains behind them. It was so picturesque it nearly stole my breath away.

"It's fabulous, Tim. I had no idea the ranch would be so beautiful." I continued gaping as he parked the pickup and turned off the ignition. There was a big barn, outbuildings, and a few horses in a corral.

While I fumbled to unfasten my seatbelt, Tim hurried around the pickup and opened my door. "Welcome to Aspen Grove Ranch," he said with a smile that made my insides begin to flutter.

## *Chapter Four*

Hesitant to take the hand he held out to me, I finally placed my palm against Tim's and braced for the sizzle I knew would strike the moment we touched. I was surprised Nancy couldn't see the sparks in the house and wonder what had caught fire in her front yard.

I slid out of the pickup then grabbed the gift basket I'd brought along as well as my purse. Tim closed the door and motioned toward the house.

"Nana is gonna be so happy you came. Let's head inside." He started down the sidewalk and I hustled to keep step with him, but came to a halt when a dog the size of a pony loped around the corner of the house and raced toward us. The oversized canine stopped just short of plowing into

Tim then dropped onto his hindquarters. His mouth was open in what almost looked like a smile and his ears perked forward. Even I could tell he was happy to see the cowboy.

"Hey, boy. What are you doing? Huh? Are you being good?" Tim reached out and rubbed a hand over the dog's head then scratched what looked like a lion's ruff. The dog leaned against him and grunted, as though he'd been waiting all day for Tim to pay him attention. When the canine noticed me standing a few feet away, he tipped his head and gave me a long, studying glance.

"Carol, I'd like you to meet Brutus. He may look like he could tear your arm off and eat it for lunch, but he's really a pretty loveable guy."

I took a step closer to the dog and waited as he sniffed me. No doubt he was getting a nose full of Hemi's scent. When he licked my fingers, I knew it was safe to pet him and gave him a few good pats. The dog was huge, furry, and had a loveable face. His breed seemed familiar, but I couldn't place it at the moment.

"What is he?" I asked, looking up at Tim as I continued rubbing Brutus' head.

"Leonberger. The breed originated in…"

"Germany," I said before Tim could finish his sentence. At his surprised look, I smiled. "I spent some time there and remember seeing a few of these dogs. They are great family dogs, aren't they?"

Tim nodded, clearly shocked I knew anything about Leonberger dogs. "That's right. They make an intimidating guard dog, drool a lot, and shed everywhere, but they're affectionate with family."

"So how did you come to have Brutus?" I asked, curious how a dog like Brutus ended up on a ranch in Montana.

"I had an Army buddy who got Brutus when he was weaned from his mama. My friend got an unexpected transfer and couldn't take the puppy with him, so I offered to keep Brutus." He ruffled a hand over the dog's ears, making Brutus' tongue hang out as he enjoyed the attention. "It looks like Brutus has declared you part of the family. He usually takes a while to warm up to strangers."

"So does Hemi, but he likes you for reasons I can't begin to understand." After I said the words, I wished I hadn't. I don't know why I kept trying to insult the guy. He had been mostly nice to me, even after I attacked him.

"Touché," Tim said, then led the way inside the house. He took my coat and hung it on a rack by the door, removed his coat and hat, then indicated I should follow him.

I was so busy admiring the gleaming wood in the entry, Tim had to take my elbow in his hand and guide me down the hallway. Although I expected the interior of the house to be dark, strategically placed windows allowed light to flood inside.

When we stepped into the great room, I sucked in a gasp. Banks of windows flanked a two-story stone fireplace and provided a magnificent view of the mountains in the background. A sea of fat red and white cattle grazed in the foreground. The scene looked like something that should be captured in a painting.

I shifted my gaze from the great outdoors to the room. Large leather chairs and couches were grouped around the fireplace. The walls along both sides of the room were lined with bookshelves and filled with not only books but also antiques and interesting pieces of art.

"What do you think?" Tim asked as he moved farther into the welcoming space.

"I think it's spectacular. The views…" I struggled to come up with words adequate to describe the sight before me, which never happened. If he'd turned me around, marched me out the door, and returned me to town at that moment, the trip still would have been well worth it just to see the stunning view.

"This is my favorite place to end the day. When the sun sets, it looks like the mountain is ablaze with color," he said. Surprised he shared something personal like that with me, I nodded my head as I continued gawking at the amazing home.

He took my elbow again and we left the room, continuing down the hallway until it opened into a bright, cheerful kitchen. Rather than log walls, it had been drywalled and painted a sunny yellow hue. Plump cushions on the chairs and matching chintz curtains at the windows gave it a homey, inviting atmosphere. Nancy sat at the kitchen table, chopping vegetables for a salad while a woman who closely resembled her, although younger, stood at the counter, basting a turkey.

"Oh, you came!" Nancy exclaimed when she saw us walk into the room.

I hurried over to her before she could try to get

up from the chair and hugged her shoulders. "How are you doing?"

"Pretty well, for a cranky old woman with a new hip," Nancy said with a grin. She pointed to the woman with the turkey baster. "Carol, I'd like you to meet my sister, Charli Presley. Charli, this is Carol Bennett. Like I mentioned, she took over Rudolph's Reads and has done great things with the store."

"It's very nice to meet you, Ms. Presley," I said, smiling at Nancy's sister.

"Call me Charli. I'm glad you could join us, Carol. I hope we didn't interrupt your plans for the day." Charli slid the turkey back in the oven and wiped her hands on a bandana-print apron.

"Not at all. I appreciate the invitation. It was so kind of you to think of me." I smiled at Nancy then handed her the basket of tea and chocolates.

"Is this that delicious tea you served when you hosted the book club in September?" she asked, holding up a box of pumpkin tea.

"The very one," I said, glad to know she'd liked it enough she remembered it months later.

"And a book!" she exclaimed, pulling it from the basket. "I'll enjoy this immensely, Carol. Thank you for your thoughtfulness."

"And thank you for yours." I patted her shoulder then looked at Charli. "Is there anything I can do to help? I'm not much of a cook, but I can cut, chop, set the table, whatever you need."

"Mash potatoes?" Charli asked.

I grinned. "I can handle that." I'd taken two steps toward her when I heard Nancy gasp. Charli and I both looked over to see her holding Tim's chin in her hand.

"Good heavens, honey. What in the world happened to you?" Nancy brushed a thumb over the cut on his cheek.

"I wasn't paying attention to what I was doing and ran into something. It'll be fine," he said, giving me a glance that said he wasn't about to admit he'd been pummeled by a girl. He hadn't lied to Nancy, though. Had he been paying attention to what he was doing he never would have snuck up my stairs and ran into my flying fists and feet, or the sconce on the wall.

"Here, Tim. Get some ice on that bruise," Charli said, taking an ice pack from the freezer. She wrapped it in a clean dishtowel and handed it to him.

Tim appeared reluctant as he took it, but I heard him sigh as he sank into a chair across the table from Nancy.

I pushed up the sleeves of my sweater, tied on the apron Charli handed to me, and started mashing potatoes. Thirty minutes later, I set the last bowl of food on the table in a glorious dining room. Tim held out a seat for me beside him. Nancy was already seated at the head of the table and Charli at the other end. Across from me, two cowboys so young they looked like they weren't yet old enough to shave shifted on their chairs and glanced at the variety of silverware placed around their plates.

Tim introduced them as Ross and Derek, although I wasn't sure which was which. Next to them, sitting by Charli, was their ranch foreman, an older man named Jack with a twinkle in his eye and a big handlebar mustache that curled into circles on the ends. From what I could see, Jack was quite taken with Charli and the feeling appeared to be mutual. I wondered if Nancy and Tim knew there was a romance simmering in their midst.

Nancy placed her hand on Tim's arm and he looked around the table. "Let's give thanks for this fine meal Aunt Charli prepared."

Tim asked a blessing that was heartfelt and the food was passed around the table.

I took pity on Ross and Derek, who had no idea which fork to pick up, and gave them silent direction. My taste buds were elated as I sampled one wonderful dish after another. Charli had prepared a golden, crisp-skinned, juicy turkey with sage stuffing that was the best I've ever eaten. In addition to the potatoes I mashed, we enjoyed creamy gravy, buttered corn, green beans seasoned with bits of onion and bacon, a green salad, cranberries accented with candied orange peel, a casserole made of broccoli and three kinds of cheese, hot rolls, and huckleberry jam.

The food was so wonderful I ate like a farmhand who'd been out in the fields all day. I'd just finished the last bite of a roll slathered with jam when Nancy cleared her throat.

"While we give that fantastic meal time to settle so we'll have room for dessert, I want everyone to say one thing they are thankful for today." Nancy looked at Tim. "You start, honey."

Tim's head moved slightly my way then he looked back at his grandmother. "I'm grateful for this warm, comfortable home, for plenty of good food to eat, for dedicated hands who work here, for friends and loved ones, for the ranch and all it provides for us, and for Nana, who keeps me on the straight and narrow." Tim glanced at me again. "And I'm really thankful I didn't run into something bigger this morning or I would have spent the day at the hospital."

Everyone laughed but I felt heat stinging my cheeks in embarrassment. Even if no one else knew what had happened to Tim's poor face, I did.

His leg bumped mine beneath the table and I jumped like I'd been zapped with a cattle prod. To cover my surprise, I smiled at the group. "I guess it's my turn. I'm thankful for kind friends who open up their home with warmth and love, and to Charli for this divine meal. I'm grateful to Tim for driving into town to get me, and I'm deeply sorry he ran into something."

He nodded at me as Charli took her turn.

When everyone had shared what they were grateful for, the men insisted on doing the dishes. Charli and I helped Nancy into the great room where she settled into a chair near the fireplace. Charli flicked a switch and flames sputtered to life, creating an amber glow that was too inviting to resist. I took a seat on the couch across from Nancy, basking in the warmth coming from the fireplace.

The two women asked me about the store, if I was ready for tomorrow's shoppers, and any holiday books they should add to their reading lists. I questioned Charli about Chicago and the restaurants where she'd worked, keeping quiet about the fact I'd eaten at a few of them.

Nancy talked about how much she hated to be unable to do her usual preparations for the holidays. Charli assured her she would do whatever she could to help.

Then my mouth got ahead of my brain, and I volunteered my services. "Anytime I can be of assistance, all you need to do is call, Nancy. The store closes at six. I have time most evenings if you need something. Or my Sunday afternoons are free."

"That's so sweet of you to offer, Carol. I would hate to bother you, knowing how hard you work. You are in that store such long hours and hardly have any time for yourself." Nancy shook her head. "A pretty young thing like you should be out living life and enjoying these carefree years."

Enjoying the carefree years and living life had resulted in my need to retreat to Christmas Mountain.

Before I came up with an appropriate reply to her comment, the men appeared and took seats. I couldn't decide if I should be happy or irritated Tim sat next to me. His masculine scent taunted my nose while his warmth penetrated my side. If he was my type, which he so completely and totally was not, I might have scooted closer to him and enjoyed his presence.

As it was, I did my best to ignore him as the group talked about the ranch, the holiday season, and things taking place in Christmas Mountain like the annual tree lighting.

An hour later, Charli served dessert with the

kind of coffee I missed from my travels in Europe. It was impossible to decide between pumpkin cheesecake with caramel sauce, apple pie with ice cream, or a flourless chocolate cake covered in a dark ganache, so I opted for a tiny piece of all three.

They were so good I had a hard time not moaning in pleasure. The chocolate cake and the coffee were a perfect pairing. I thought I caught hints of hazelnut in the coffee as I took another sip. Normally, I preferred tea, but once in a while, there was just something about a ridiculously good cup of coffee that couldn't be beat. Like now.

Tim must have sensed my enjoyment of dessert and coffee because when he caught my eye, he had a lopsided grin on his face that made my heart skip a few beats. What was it about hunky men and cute grins that caused a woman's brain cells to deplete at warp speed?

"I think Carol is enjoying dessert, Aunt Charli," he said, giving me a teasing wink.

"It's beyond delicious, Charli. Thank you for all the work you put into this spectacular meal."

Charli flapped a hand my direction. "It was nothing, Carol. I love to cook and enjoy baking."

"And the worst part is that she whipped all this up in the time it would have taken me to get the turkey in the oven and make the pie," Nancy said, giving her sister a disgusted look.

The conversation was light and pleasant as we finished our dessert. Everyone but Nancy helped with the dishes and putting dessert away.

"Since you're here, would you like to see a little of the ranch?" Tim asked, looking at me.

"I'd love to, if you're sure you don't mind showing me around." I still wasn't sure where I stood with Tim, or even if I'd decided he was a friend instead of a foe. But I really wanted to see the ranch.

"Come on," he said, leading the way to a large laundry room off the kitchen. Chore coats hung on hooks and boots in various stages of scuffed, dirty, and coated in mud sat on a rubber mat on the floor. He lifted a tan canvas coat from a hook and held it for me. "Wear one of Nana's coats. That way you won't have to worry about ruining yours."

"Thank you," I said, slipping my arms in the sleeves that were a few inches too short, but not bad, all things considered. The coat was a little big in circumference, but it was warm, and that was the important thing.

"There should be gloves in the pockets," Tim said as he shrugged into a coat that had seen better days, but appeared clean.

I pulled out a pair of leather work gloves and slipped them on as we walked out the back door and down the steps.

He gave me a tour of the barn, pointed out the bunkhouse and other outbuildings, and stopped at a corral so I could pet a beautiful bay horse.

"Rowan likes you," he said as I ran a hand over the horse's neck.

"The feeling is mutual. Yours?" I asked.

He nodded, then took an apple from his pocket. Amazed, I watched as he broke it in two with his bare hands. He handed me half of it. "If you feed him, you'll have a friend for life."

Gingerly, I held out the apple to Rowan. When he muzzled it from my hand, I smiled so broadly, my cheeks hurt. Tim dropped the other half in my hand and Rowan gladly took it from me.

"Thank you for that, Tim," I said as we headed in the direction of the house. Brutus walked with us while two cow dogs napped at the top of the bunkhouse steps. I couldn't seem to keep my hands off of Brutus' soft fur. Since his head came up to almost my waist, it wasn't hard to reach out and pet him.

As we walked, Tim pointed out a treehouse his great-grandfather had built, a sign his great-aunt had painted, and tractor he'd helped his grandpa restore when he was home on leave the year before Bill passed away.

We were almost up the house steps when the door opened and Ross, Derek, and Jack trooped outside. All three men removed their hats and tipped their heads politely.

"It was a pleasure to meet you, Carol. I hope you'll come out and visit us again," Jack said with a grin that made his mustache twitch.

"I enjoyed meeting all of you, too. Thank you for making me feel welcome today." I smiled at each of them.

"Come back anytime," Ross said, or maybe it was Derek. The other one rapidly nodded his head.

I gave them another smile before Tim escorted me inside the house. As he helped me out of his grandmother's chore coat, his fingers brushed against my neck and I fought down a shiver generated by the brief touch. What was it about this guy that affected me so?

And it couldn't all be attributed to a gorgeous smile and hunky body. I wasn't that shallow.

"I should probably get back," I said, although I had thoroughly enjoyed my time at the ranch.

"Are you sure you don't want to stay for supper? Aunt Charli's serving leftovers."

Thoughts of more fabulous food were almost enough to change my mind, but not quite. I wasn't sure how much time around Tim I could handle before I gave in to one of the loony urges racing through my mind to give him a hug, or a kiss, or cuddle on the couch with his fingers entwined with mine.

Yep. Definitely time to go.

We walked into the kitchen to find Nancy and Charli at the table with newspaper ads spread out around them.

Tim groaned. "Please tell me the two of you aren't thinking about driving somewhere to shop tomorrow? Nana, you know you can't do that with your hip."

Both women glared at him like he was a few bricks shy of a whole wall.

"You won't believe it, honey," Nancy said in a syrupy tone. "But they have this modern marvel called a computer that lets you shop online from the comfort of your own home."

From the corner of my eye, I watched Tim start to say something then snap his mouth shut at his grandmother's sarcasm. "Okay, Nana. Shop all you want. Carol is ready to go so I'm gonna take her home."

"Oh, must you leave so soon, darling?" Nancy asked, holding out a hand to me.

I took it between mine and gave it a gentle pat. "You all have been so gracious and kind and I appreciate it more than you can know, but I've got a super busy day tomorrow, so I better get home. Thank you, again, for inviting me today. It's the nicest Thanksgiving I've had in a long, long time."

Nancy squeezed my hand and smiled. "You come anytime you want, Carol. We'd love to have you. I hope you do great tomorrow."

"Me, too," I said, then turned to Charli. "It was fabulous to meet you and thank you for the best food I've eaten since I can't even tell you when."

"You are most welcome." Charli hopped up and hurried over to the massive refrigerator. "Let me send you home with leftovers."

"Oh, I couldn't," I said. I'd already crashed their holiday after beating on Tim. I wouldn't feel right taking more.

"I insist. We've got enough leftovers in here to last for days. You get your coat while I put a few things together." Charli smiled at me as she took bowls out of the fridge and set them on the counter. "It's no trouble at all."

"Don't argue with her," Tim whispered in my ear. When his breath, warm and smelling slightly of mint, caressed my neck it made tingles roll from my head to my toes.

Slightly dazed, I allowed him to lead me back to the front door where I'd left my coat and purse. He held my coat for me like a perfect gentleman. As I fastened the buttons, he grabbed his coat then hurried down the hall toward the kitchen. He wasn't gone long when he returned with a bag full of plastic food containers.

"No. That's way too much," I said, reaching for the bag as I walked to the kitchen.

He grabbed my arm, pulling me to a stop in the hall. "Just take it. You've made Nana so happy by coming and Aunt Charli loves to cook. Seriously, take the food and enjoy it."

I would have argued, but when I looked into his eyes, all I could think about was delectable chocolate. Mutely, I nodded my head and let him guide me out the door and down the steps.

We were almost to the highway when I felt the need to break the silence that fell between us.

"Nancy's never mentioned your parents. Where do they live?"

His jaw tightened and I caught a hint of a wince. I wasn't sure if it was because of the bruise from where I kicked him or thoughts of his parents.

"Forget I asked. My curiosity gets the best of me sometimes," I said, sounding lame even to my own ears.

"No, it's okay. My mom was never into the ranching thing, but she had her life goals planned out by the time she was ten. She graduated from high school with honors, attended Harvard, became a doctor, and has a booming obstetrics practice. Mom met Dad in college. He's a corporate attorney who works almost as many hours as Mom. Growing up, I had a nanny, rarely saw my parents, and spent all my vacation time at the ranch with Nana and Pops. My parents nearly disowned me when I joined the service instead of going to college, but they eventually got over it. They still live in Washington D.C. and rarely visit. They came for my grandpa's funeral, but that was the last time we've seen them. I know it breaks Nana's heart, but she hides it well."

Wow. It looked like I wasn't the only one with issues.

"I'm sorry, Tim. I know what it's like to be at odds with a parent."

One of his dark eyebrows winged upward. "You do?"

I nodded, wishing I hadn't said anything. Of course, anyone who knew me from my childhood years had witnessed firsthand the agony visited upon me by Darcy Ledford Bennett, my mother.

"By the time I was three, my mother decided what she wanted me to be when I grew up and set about making it happen. Unfortunately, her plans and mine were galaxies apart. After I lost my dad, things between us fell completely apart. I haven't spoken to her in years."

"I'm sorry, Carol. That's rough." His hand slid across the seat and clasped mine. Warmth unlike anything I'd ever experienced flooded through me. "How old were you when your dad passed away?" he asked.

"Eighteen. It was right before I graduated from high school." I sighed and looked out the window. "Dad was brilliant and fun and wonderful. Any good memories I have from my childhood are because of him. He was a wildlife technician. His job is the reason we moved to Christmas Mountain when I was four. Before that, we lived in California, but I don't remember much about it. Mom hated it here, but she's a freelance grant writer and can work from anywhere. The morning after I graduated, I packed my car and left town. My mother threatened any number of dire consequences, but when it came down to it, I was an adult and could make my own choices."

"That must have been hard, to leave like that, and so soon after losing your father."

The sympathy in Tim's eyes wasn't helping my emotional state. However, I had lots of practice at shoving down a lump in my throat and acting like everything was fine. "It was hard, but I survived."

"When was the last time you spoke with your mother?"

I picked at a non-existent piece of lint on my sweater. The last conversation I had with my mom wasn't pleasant. Horrific would be a better description, but the little bit of sharing my past with Tim made me feel marginally better than I had in a while. "I've spoken to her twice in the last nine years. I called her a few days after I left home to let her know I was fine. Because she sounded so cold when she finally stopped yelling at me, I told her I got a job at a truck stop as a waitress and had found my true calling. She hung up on me."

Tim grinned. "Was any of it true?"

I shook my head. "No. I was at a truck stop eating breakfast at the time and I did eventually spend a month working as a waitress, but it is definitely not my true calling."

His grin broadened. "What about the next time

you talked to her?"

"That was four years ago. I was…" I paused. I couldn't exactly tell him where I'd been or why I was there or all my efforts to leave the past behind me would be in vain. "I was shocked to hear from her. She was getting married and invited me to the wedding."

"Did you go?"

"No. No I did not, and because of that, I don't think she'll ever forgive me. I received a scathing letter in the mail after the wedding letting me know she'd disowned me and never wanted to hear from me again."

"I'm sorry, Carol. No parent should be that way. It's just wrong in so many ways."

The lump I'd managed to tamp down earlier was about to completely fill my throat. Not only that, but I felt tears stinging the backs of my eyes. I forced my thoughts to happy things. To my store. To Hemi. To Christmas. To good-looking cowboys with hearts made of marshmallows.

That last one almost made me smile and the lump receded, allowing me to breathe.

I glanced up and realized Tim was almost to Rudolph's Reads. He didn't bother to park in one of the clearly outlined spaces, instead pulling up parallel to the curb. Since there wasn't another car to be seen in the entire block, I didn't think anyone would mind.

He started to cut the ignition, but I grabbed his hand. "Don't bother getting out, I can see myself inside. Thank you for today, for coming to get me, bringing me home, and showing me the ranch. And for being nice even when I clobbered you."

"I don't know about clobbered," he said with a frown although his eyes smiled. "It was my pleasure, Carol. You really are welcome at the ranch anytime. Nana would love to see you, and Aunt Charli would too."

I wanted to ask if he'd be happy to see me, but refrained. Quickly gathering my things, I had my hand on the door handle, when something overtook me. Call it a loss of all sense. Call it a turkey hangover. Call it the need to feel connected to another human. Whatever the reason, I leaned over and kissed Tim's cheek, the one I hadn't accidentally scratched in the throes of my ninja impersonation.

One moment he was staring at me, confused. The next, his arms were around me and his lips captured mine.

Caught off guard, I didn't push him away. Rather, my hand slid up his arm and around his shoulder. His kiss started out gentle and sweet, and he tasted like spearmint gum blended with something dark and dangerous. The combination was about to prove lethal to my system.

The kiss deepened, gained intensity, and bright sparks of light exploded behind my eyes. I could have happily remained with his lips locked to mine for eternity. Then the reality of where I was and what I was doing slammed into me with the force of a freight train.

With a jerk, I pulled back.

At the wounded look on his face, I placed a quick kiss on that seductive mouth and hopped out of the pickup before I found myself necking with him in front of the store like we were sixteen with rampaging hormones.

"Thanks, Tim. Have a nice evening." I shut the pickup door and unlocked my front door. He didn't pull away from the curb until I was safely inside the store. I managed to walk upstairs, put away the leftovers, and sink onto my couch before my legs began to shake.

Tim Burke might be opinionated and way too perceptive, but he was definitely a phenomenal kisser.

## *Chapter Five*

Miracles happened in Christmas Mountain because I somehow survived Black Friday and Small Business Saturday without losing my mind. In fact, the store had been so busy, I hired one of Josie's friends to help out through Christmas.

People loved our book tree, the elf in the window, and all the decorations that made the store a festive place to visit. Rather than serve coffee, I filled the pot with hot spiced cider each day. And Christmas carols played on a continuous loop, which made me deliriously happy.

Karen had the great idea to set up a gift-wrapping area so we could offer customers free gift-wrapping for in-store purchases or charge for gifts purchased elsewhere. We put up a sign that all funds collected would be donated to purchase toys and clothes for needy children in our community.

Aiden hated wrapping gifts, but the rest of us got into it and had a lot of fun creating pretty packages. I could just imagine them nestled under a tree, waiting for the recipient to claim them Christmas morning.

Multiple times, I'd thought about calling Aspen Grove Ranch to see how Nancy was doing. Okay, fine. I admit it. It wasn't just Nancy I wanted to connect with. I wanted to check up on Tim. After that sizzling kiss Thanksgiving evening, I couldn't get him out of my mind. Maybe we had a few missteps at our first meeting, and that whole Karate Kid moment was definitely a strike against me, but I'd enjoyed his company. Especially when his lips captured mine.

Thoughts of that kiss nearly drove me crazy. Convinced it hadn't affected him at all, I assumed that was the reason I hadn't heard from him. With Christmas rapidly approaching it was probably for the best. I just needed to survive what was turning out to be a stellar season for my business. I'd taken four steps toward the Christmas section at the front of the store to restock a selection of Christmas cards when I bumped into my friend Joy and her son, Max.

"Hey, what brings you into Rudolph's Reads?" I asked as I gave Joy a hug and smiled at Max.

"Just a little shopping," Joy said, perusing a table of sale items Josie had arranged the previous evening.

"If there's something you're looking for

specifically, let me know. If you don't see it out here, I might have it back in the storage room. We've had trouble keeping the shelves stocked recently."

Joy grinned. "I'm so happy for you, Carol. It's wonderful to see the store doing so well. You've brought new life to it."

"Thank you. I feel like here is where I'm meant to be."

She nodded and glanced at Max who looked thoroughly bored.

"Do you mind if I borrow Max for a few minutes? I just got some new books and I'd like his opinion on them."

Joy looked at her son. "What do you think, Max? Go with Carol or hang out with me while I shop."

"Carol," he said, grinning at his mother.

"Take as long as you need to shop, Joy. I can keep him busy," I whispered as I motioned for Max to walk with me to the children's section.

After showing him two new books about galaxies and outer space geared specifically for children, he plopped down in a chair and started reading. I straightened shelves and helped a man searching for a book about traveling to Germany find what he was looking for, all while keeping an eye on Max.

Twenty minutes later, my phone chimed and I took it out of my pocket. Joy was at the cash register, ready to go.

"I think your mom is ready to leave," I said to Max. Reverently, he set the books back on the shelf where I'd taken them from and followed me to the front of the store. I'd make sure Auntie Carol wrapped up those books as his Christmas gift.

Joy mouthed "thank you" when I approached the counter, took Max's hand, and left the store.

"It was nice to give her time to shop without a child underfoot," Karen said as she handed another customer their purchase.

"Max is a great kid." And he was. Before I could give any thought to my lack of children and no hope for any arriving in my near or distant future, I went back to stocking shelves.

The bell above the door jingled, then I heard something jangle. I'd been setting out a new shipment of romance books, but I quickly stacked them on the floor and peeked around the end of the aisle.

There, in all his cowboy glory, was Tim Burke. Beside him, Nancy leaned on a walker, glancing around with a look of wonder on her face.

"Nancy! What are you doing out and about?" I asked as I hurried over to her and gave her a hug.

"I had to get out and do something. Being cooped up was about to drive me batty," she said, unwrapping the scarf around her neck then stuffing gloves into her coat pockets. "The store looks marvelous, Carol. I've never seen it so festive and welcoming." She drew in a deep breath. "It even smells like Christmas."

I'd gone to great lengths to plug in holiday air fresheners throughout the store so the moment someone stepped inside, it truly did smell like home and holidays and sweet memories all wrapped up together. The spices in the hot cider mingled with the smell of books as an underlying, pleasant fragrance.

However, standing this close to Tim, all I could smell was his manly, outdoorsy scent. Not that I was totally against it. Not at all.

While Nancy chatted about the decorations and displays, I cast a covert glance at Tim. The scratch on his cheek had healed and the bruising on his jaw had turned to a pale shade of yellow. He really had been a good sport about the whole thing. Looking back, he could have used brute force to subdue me before I got in quite so many kicks and hits, but I'd probably caught him totally unaware.

Hemi wandered out front and twined around Tim's legs as he stood next to his grandmother.

"Hey, Hemi, my man. How are you?" Tim picked up the cat and stroked his fur.

Hemi's motor revved and took off at a rapid clip, making me smile.

"He won't even let me pet him," Karen said as she breezed past us with an armload of travel books. "I'm Karen, one of Carol's minions."

Tim grinned and tipped his hat. "Tim Burke. I assume you know my grandmother."

"Of course," Karen said with a friendly smile. "We all love Nancy."

"And I love you all right back," Nancy said. She placed a hand on my arm and pointed to a table with three chairs near the biography section. "Do you think I could sit down and have a cup of that cider I smell?"

"You most certainly may. Want anything to

read?" I asked, walking with her as she slowly made her way to the table. Tim helped her into a chair then set her walker behind her. "Mmm. Let me think while you get that cider."

I hurried to fill two cups, handing one to her and the other to Tim. He took his with a nod. I tried not to grin at him. He looked like he'd rather be anywhere else than in the middle of the bookstore on a busy afternoon.

"Didn't I see there's a new book out by that gal who writes the western romances I like?" Nancy asked as she sipped the cider.

"Yes. In fact, I was just putting those books on the shelf. I'll grab one and you can take a look." I rushed over to the romance section and snagged the book in question. I walked around the end of the aisle and smacked into a solid wall of man at the beginning of the Christmas display.

"Fancy meeting you like this," Tim whispered as his hands settled on my arms, holding me upright and so very close.

Unnerved by his proximity, I didn't even protest when he tugged me through the holiday display and into the hallway that led to the storeroom. Away from prying eyes, he stopped halfway to the storage room.

His thumb brushed across my cheek as his gaze fused to mine. Mercy! How was a girl supposed to keep her head on straight when six and a half feet of rugged, incredible male was standing toe to toe with her?

I finally gathered enough sense to speak. "What are you doing?"

"Just saying hello." His voice was a husky rumble that made my insides quiver. It was a sensation I'd never experienced and I didn't even have enough wits left to decide if I liked it or not.

"Hello," I said softly, unable to do anything except continue staring at him. Not that I wanted to. Something in the chocolate depths of his eyes spoke to my heart in a way words never could.

"I was wondering if you might have some suggestions for a gift for Nana?" His question made complete sense as to why he'd want to corner me away from his grandmother. However, the way his hands rubbed tantalizing circles along my back made no sense at all. At least none my addled brain could comprehend at the moment.

"I could come up with some ideas. Do you need the gift today?" I asked.

"No. I'll come in one day without her along and do some shopping. Maybe, if you aren't too busy, we could have lunch or dinner or something."

Lunch or dinner or something, particularly if the something included a few more scorching kisses, sounded fabulous. Perhaps I should play hard to get. I definitely wouldn't let him know I was so attracted to him I hadn't been able to get a solid night of sleep since Thanksgiving because I kept dreaming of him.

"I'll have to check my schedule..." At his crestfallen look, I hastened onward. "But I'm sure we can figure something out."

He appeared relieved then the next thing I knew, his lips brushed over mine. It happened so quickly, I wasn't entirely sure I hadn't imagined it.

My heart stuttered then began to race as he pulled back with a grin.

Before I did something entirely ridiculous, like throw myself at the cowboy who smiled at me with such warmth in his incredible eyes, I turned away from him and made my way to Nancy, gave her the book in my hand, then went to help Karen at the cash register.

Ten minutes later, Tim carried several books to the counter and I rang them up while Nancy continued sitting at the table, sipping cider.

"Are these all for Nancy?" I asked, noticing a variety of genres she normally didn't read.

"No. Christmas gifts," Tim said, handing me cash to pay for the purchase.

"In that case, would you like them wrapped?"

He shook his head. "I think she wants to do it. Wrapping is something she can do sitting at the table. She's been whining as bad as a cranky five-year-old about not being able to hang lights and deck the halls this year. I told her she should have thought of that before she decided to have surgery right before the holidays."

I smiled and handed him the bag with the books. "I'm sure it's hard on her, but so nice Charli could come to stay. Will she return to Chicago soon?"

Tim shrugged. "That remains to be seen. I don't know if you noticed, but she and Jack can't stop making moony-eyes at each other."

"I did pick up on that," I said, walking with him over to where Nancy slowly got to her feet, pulled on her gloves, and prepared to leave. I gave her a hug and she kissed my cheek.

"If you don't have anything better to do, why don't you come to the ranch for lunch this Sunday and spend the afternoon?" Nancy asked as she slowly shuffled to the door.

"Oh, I couldn't impose on you like that, Nancy. I still feel bad about crashing your family Thanksgiving."

She gave me a long, serious look. "You didn't crash anything. I invited you and sent Timothy to get you. If we didn't want your company, he sure wouldn't have driven into town to pick you up. Please just think about coming out. You don't have to let me know right away. You could even make it a last-minute decision and call when you're on your way."

"I'll think about it." And I would. I loved the idea of getting out of town and hanging at the ranch for an afternoon, but I certainly didn't want to make a pest of myself. When Tim winked at me as he held the door for Nancy, I knew unless we had a blizzard, I'd head out to the ranch after church.

The day flew by and it wasn't until five that I noticed an occupant in my special reading alcove. The girl was probably around thirteen with short, purple hair. It looked as though she'd randomly whacked it with a pair of rusty scissors since it stuck up in some places and other pieces were longer with the slightest hint of a curl.

Her face was oval, her skin like porcelain, and she had the biggest, prettiest green eyes I'd ever seen when she looked up at me and scowled. A used copy of *The Goose Girl* was open on her lap as she sat cross-legged on the pillows in the alcove.

"May I help you with anything?" I asked.

"No, I'm fine." Her gaze dropped back to the book.

"If you need anything please let me know." I left her there, but made a note to check to see if she lingered right up until closing time. Vaguely, I recalled seeing her walk in around the time Josie arrived for work, which was right after school. In fact, I'd noticed a purple head in my store a few times, and wondered if it had been the same girl.

I'd definitely keep an eye on her. She reminded me of my younger self with that scared, wounded look on her face. If there was a way I could help her, I wanted to do it. After all, if it wasn't for Mr. Abernathy and his kindness, who knew what would have become of me.

Later that evening, I'd just settled into my favorite chair with a cup of chamomile tea and a good book when my phone rang.

"Hi, Joy. Is the little man already in bed?" I asked, realizing it was past her son's bedtime.

"Tucked in and asleep," Joy said, sounding tired.

"Rough day?" I asked then took a sip from the steaming cup of tea.

"Exhausting."

I smiled. "Maybe you need to find some handsome guy willing to come over and rub your feet or massage your neck."

"If you're going to be that way, I'll hang up," she said in warning.

"Don't do that. I'll behave. Did Max have fun

at school today?"

She shared a few tidbits from Max's day and hers. "I heard Nancy Wright was in your store today along with her hunky grandson. I thought you'd declared he was a boorish buffoon and would never speak to him again. The grapevine gossip said you couldn't keep your eyes off him."

I would have choked on my tea if I'd just taken a sip. "What?"

Joy laughed. "Would it be so terrible to go on a date with a good-looking guy who, from all reports, is exceptionally kind and caring with his grandmother?"

"Why don't you go out with him and let me know?"

Another laugh clued me in to my friend's amusement. "No, thank you. I've got enough trouble with men without borrowing any from you."

Before I could ask questions, Joy changed the topic to The Christmas Extravaganza planned for Christmas evening at the community center. There were seven of us who would perform in a tribute to our beloved teacher, Ms. King. We chatted a few more minutes then I heard Joy attempt to stifle a yawn.

"I better let you get to bed, Joy. I'm so glad you called, though."

"I'm glad I did, too. Sleep well and dream of that cutie cowboy of yours."

"He is most certainly not mine and I never said he was cute."

"Nope, but I could tell you're thinking it," she teased.

"Get some rest," I said, unable to resist the opportunity to goad her a bit. "Maybe I could ask Tim if he has any friends who'd be willing to come over and make you some hot cocoa and read you a bedtime story."

"That's enough out of you. Sweet dreams."

After I hung up with Joy, I couldn't concentrate on the book I'd been reading. Not when thoughts of Tim continually filled my head.

## *Chapter Six*

Exhausted after a long day of helping customers in the store, I was too tired to haul the trash out into the chilly night air. All I wanted was something to eat and the warm comfort of my bed. I left the trash bagged by the back door with a promise to myself to take it out first thing the next morning.

Bright and early, I opened the door, and let Hemi out into the chilly morning darkness. Quickly grabbing the bags of trash, I trudged down the alley as the frosty air threatened to freeze the inside of my nose and made me wish I'd taken the time to yank on a coat. My eyes watered at the frigid temperature, but I blinked away the moisture and lifted the lid on the dumpster. Hastily tossing the bags inside, I returned to the door and stopped, breathing in the clean mountain air. Someone was cooking bacon and the aroma made my stomach growl. As soon as I fed the cat, I fully intended to go upstairs and make myself a decent breakfast.

"Hemi!" I called since the cat had disappeared goodness only knew where. "Hemi! Come on boy." Still nothing.

I walked to the other end of the alley, grateful for the lights on the surrounding buildings, but Hemi was nowhere to be seen. Maybe he'd dashed back inside when I wasn't looking. I turned around and took a step toward my still open door when a hand wrapped around my arm and pulled me back.

Out of pure reflex, I rammed my elbow into my assailant's stomach, stomped on his foot, and screamed like Jack the Ripper had me in his clutches.

"Carol!"

I recognized that masculine voice. In fact, the sound of it sent shivers down my spine and caused me to whip around. Tim stood nearby, bent slightly forward with one hand pressed to his midsection and the other holding Hemi. Once again, I'd attacked him in a state of panic.

"Oh, my gosh! I'm so sorry, Tim." I didn't know what to do, other than apologize.

"No worries," he said, handing me the cat. "I really do need to learn not to sneak up on you."

"Well, that would be a good start." I smiled at him. "What are you doing in town so early?"

"I had to come to the feed store. Since it doesn't open until eight, I thought I'd swing by and see if you wanted to have breakfast together." He straightened, although he kept a hand pressed to his stomach. "I knocked on the front door but you didn't answer, then I saw Hemi and followed him back here. I didn't mean to startle you. So would you?"

"Would I what?" I asked, leading the way inside the storeroom. I set Hemi down then locked the door after Tim closed it behind him.

"Have breakfast with me, unless you've already eaten."

Dare I go out to eat with Tim? Would it set tongues wagging? Would I have a deluge of calls wanting to know who he was and why my friends hadn't heard about him?

The answer to all three questions was yes, but I decided he was worth battling any gossip that might arise.

"I'd love to have breakfast with you. What do you have in mind?" I poured food into Hemi's bowl then glanced up at Tim.

"Prancer's Pancake House sound okay to you?"

"Sounds great." I got Hemi a bowl of fresh water, washed my hands, then motioned toward the hallway. "I just need to run upstairs for my coat."

"I'll wait down here," he said, following me as far as the stairs.

I rushed into the apartment, snagged my coat and purse, grabbed my glasses, and hurried back downstairs. It was a good thing I was an early riser and was already ready for the day, otherwise, Tim might have found me in the alley in my bathrobe.

"Ready to go?" he asked, as I made my way down the creaky stairs.

"Yes." When I stepped outside, I noticed an older single cab pickup with the Aspen Grove Ranch logo emblazoned on the side. The bed of it was scratched and there was a dent by the rear fender.

"I usually drive it when I need to make a run to the feed store." Tim motioned toward the pickup. "Hope you don't mind riding in it."

"I don't mind, but why don't we walk? It's not far to Prancer's," I said. I already regretted not wrapping a scarf around my neck and covering my head with a hat. That thing they say about body heat escaping out the top of your head is true in my case. If I don't wear a hat, I'm freezing.

I wasn't exactly dressed for a jaunt in the cold as the skirt of my maxi dress floated around the black boots I'd purchased in Brazil. Although the dress I wore definitely wasn't runway fashion, it was nicer than many of the baggy clothes I wore. Black with little burgundy rosebuds sprigged across the fabric, it looked nice with my long burgundy cardigan. I slipped on my glasses, tucked my hands into my pockets, and tried not to think about Jack Frost biting not just my nose, but also my fingers and toes.

Whether he noticed my discomfort or was just being sweet I'm not certain, but Tim moved closer and dropped an arm around my shoulder.

"You looked cold," he said by way of an explanation as we continued walking in silence.

Engulfed by his presence, I went from practically hypothermic to nearly overheated in a matter of seconds.

Since it was so early in the day, there were only a few people at Prancer's when we stepped inside. As though we'd already discussed it, we both headed for a booth in the back corner.

"Ladies first," Tim said, motioning for me to choose a seat. Although I would have preferred to sit so I could keep an eye on everyone coming and going, I slid onto the bench with my back to the door.

Tim removed his hat and coat then sat across from me. "So, do you eat here often?"

"No. Not often." I liked the peace and quiet of my apartment and store. Even if I could barely do more than boil water, I wasn't big on eating out. I mostly ate salads or opened cans of soup.

The two of us were quiet as we studied the menu. Bacon was definitely going to be included with my order.

Country Christmas songs that were popular a few decades ago played from the jukebox adding the perfect touch to the quirky décor. I listened to Willie Nelson sing about pretty paper and smiled. My dad had been a huge country music fan, even if my mother couldn't abide it.

When a server approached our table to take our orders, I was lost in memories of riding along with my dad, both of us enthusiastically singing to the radio.

"Carol? Did you decide what you'd like?" Tim asked, bringing me back to the present.

"Um, yes." We placed our orders and once the server left, we fell into an easy conversation about happenings in town and how things were going at the ranch.

Ten minutes later, the server set a huge stack of pancakes in front of Tim along with another plate loaded with eggs, hash browns, and sausages. My eyes bulged at the sight of all that food.

"Hungry?" I asked, giving him a teasing grin as the waitress set a plate in front of me.

"As a matter of fact, I am." He smeared butter on his pancakes, smothered them with syrup, and sat back with a look of anticipation on his face as he cut a bite.

"Well?" I asked as I drizzled syrup on my French toast. "How are the pancakes?"

He leaned forward and dropped his voice to a whisper. "Not as good as Nana's or Aunt Charli's, but still pretty tasty." When he winked at me, I almost dropped the syrup pitcher.

While he ate what appeared to be enough food for three people, I savored my French toast, crispy bacon, and two scrambled eggs. I washed it all down with a cup of Earl Grey tea.

"I've noticed your preference for tea over coffee. Do you not drink coffee at all?" he asked, taking a drink from a cup of straight black coffee that was strong enough I couldn't even swallow it without stirring in three packets of sugar and four of cream.

I couldn't exactly admit I'd been spoiled by the most decadent coffee money could buy from all around the globe, so I shook my head.

"It has to be an awesome cup of coffee before I enjoy it. Your aunt's coffee on Thanksgiving was perfect." I raised my cup of tea. "I like tea because it takes little effort to make, comes in a variety of flavors, and is so comforting when I have time to curl up with a good book."

He eyed me as he dragged the last bite of pancake through the remaining pool of syrup on his plate. "If I had to guess, I'd say you curl up with a good book almost every day."

I shrugged, rather than admit he was right. Again. Did the Army train him in psychoanalysis or something?

"Will Nancy be able to attend the tree lighting?" I asked, desperate to shift the conversation away from me.

"No. Nana is mad at me because I told her it was a terrible idea. With snow on the ground and ice lurking around, I'm worried about her getting hurt. Aunt Charli agrees with me, but Nana has been pitching a full-fledged fit about not missing it."

"Maybe someone could record it for her," I suggested, deciding I could be the one to do it. Originally, I planned to avoid the tree lighting ceremony but Joy had talked me into attending. I'd be there with my friends, participating in the annual event. I was looking forward to spending time with Ashley, Morgan, Faith, Emma, and Joy.

Tim gave me a look that said he could convince me to go with him, so I glanced away. The noise in the restaurant increased as more people arrived, hungry for gossip and breakfast.

Miles Wilson, owner of the feed store and resident town grump (although everyone knows he's a softy under that crusty exterior) approached our table with his wild white hair giving him the appearance of a mad scientist. He kind of reminded me of Christopher Lloyd's character in the *Back to the Future* movies.

"What are you doing here?" he asked Tim, not even bothering with the niceties like "good morning" or "nice to see you."

"I need a load of feed," Tim said, smiling at the older man. "I'll be at the store when you open."

"Give me time to get my breakfast and I might even unlock the doors a few minutes early." Mr. Wilson tossed me a speculative glance. "Although I don't reckon you're in a big rush." He turned and sauntered off to his usual spot at the counter.

Out of a nervous habit, I pushed the glasses up on my nose. Tim reached over and removed them. "Why do you wear those hideous things?"

"Because…" I said, snatching them out of his hand and settling them back into place. "They aren't hideous. I'll have you know, they're expensive and the style was one of the most popular last year."

He pulled them off again and set them on the table. "They are hideous because they hide your beautiful eyes."

What did you say to a comment like that? I had no idea, so I mumbled "thank you."

"What are you hiding from, Christmas Carol?" Tim questioned. He lifted my right hand and held it between his. The snap of electricity his touch always created was still there as it zipped up my arm.

My heart felt like the syrup we'd both enjoyed for breakfast when he called me Christmas Carol.

Dad used to call me that sometimes and I'd missed it. The holidays were a horrible time to feel alone and I'd felt that way ever since my dad passed away. Sure, I had friends, but it wasn't the same. Nothing or no one could ever fill the void left by my father's death, but I was starting to realize I needed more in my life than the bookstore, the cat, and old western marathons.

Regardless, I wasn't yet ready to spill my guts to Tim. I might never be ready for that to happen and this morning in a busy restaurant was certainly not the time nor place.

Our harried server slapped the check on the table. Before I could pick it up to see what my share of breakfast totaled, Tim snatched it up.

"I'll pay for my meal," I said, digging around in my purse for my wallet.

"No, Carol. I invited you, it's my treat. Besides, in case you haven't yet figured it out, I'm kinda old-fashioned. If I go anywhere with a female, I pay for her meals, open her doors, that sort of thing. Nana would flail the skin right off me if I didn't act like a gentleman."

Rather than argue and make a scene (which would have been a nightmare come true), I gathered my things, stood, and started to slip on my coat. Tim took it from me and held it while I jammed my arms into the sleeves.

"Coat holding on that old-fashioned list, too?" I asked as he yanked on his coat, settled his cowboy hat on his head, and waited for me to walk ahead of him to the register.

"As a matter of fact, it is." He paid the bill,

waved at Miles, then we stepped outside. Fingers of light spread across the morning sky and I took a deep breath. Among the usual scents, I could smell Tim's masculine fragrance.

Annoyed even my olfactory system seemed to be attuned to him, I rubbed my finger beneath my nose and started back toward my store. "Thank you for breakfast. I appreciate it," I said as we walked across the street.

"My pleasure. Oh, and don't let me forget, Aunt Charli sent you something. It's in the pickup."

I perked up. If Charli sent it, I assumed it was food. Even though I'd just eaten what I considered a big breakfast, my mouth watered at the thought of the tasty treat she may have sent with Tim.

Then I looked over at him and my mouth watered for an entirely different reason. The morning light backlit him as he strolled down the street. His rugged profile made my heart kick into a thumping gait.

"So, what did you do in the Army?" I asked, in need of a serious distraction from my attraction to the cowboy.

"I led an infantry troop. Boots on the ground."

I had no idea what that meant. At my open look of curiosity, he appeared to consider what to say, then finally sighed in resignation. "The infantry are troops on the ground that engage with the enemy in close-range combat. We operate weapons and equipment to engage and destroy or capture the enemy. The infantry is responsible for defending our country against any threat by land."

"Oh," I said, feeling ignorant. I admire people

who serve in the military. I appreciate them far more than I'll probably ever be able to express. Yet, when it comes right down to it, I really have no idea what they do other than keep us safe and make sacrifices greater than the average person could comprehend.

I placed a hand on Tim's arm. "Thank you for your service. I'm sure what you did had to be physically and mentally demanding."

He just nodded his head and kept walking.

I don't know why I kept pestering him to tell me more about his time in the Army, but something inside me wouldn't let it rest. "If you didn't have the responsibility of the ranch, would you go back?"

He remained quiet so long, I concluded I'd pushed a little too far, but he finally shook his head. "No. Going back isn't an option, ranch or not."

A hundred additional questions fluttered inside my head, but I decided to interrogate him further another day.

"Let me get the stuff from Aunt Charli," he said as we arrived back at the store.

While I unlocked the door and hit the switch on a power strip to turn on the Christmas lights (thank you, Aiden, for making that task simple), Tim retrieved a big basket from the pickup and carried it into the store.

When he set it on the counter, a multitude of delicious scents wafted up from the red and white striped dishtowel tucked over the top. I pulled back and got a peek of muffins, croissants, cookies, and even a resealable baggie full of fudge.

Heaven. I was in heaven.

Without a lick of restraint, I pulled out a piece of fudge and took a bite. Eyes closed, I savored the smooth, rich chocolate as it coated my tongue and left me in a state of holiday candy-induced euphoria.

"So good," I moaned, taking another bite.

Tim chuckled and picked up Hemi as the cat wandered out from the back.

"Do you think she'll share, Hemi?" Tim asked, stroking the cat's fur and earning purrs for his efforts. "What's that?" he asked, holding the cat close to his ear. "According to Hemi, you will wallop anyone who gets between you and your chocolate. From the bruises I've gained since meeting you, I accept that as the truth."

I stopped indulging in the piece of fudge long enough to glance at Tim as he leaned back against the counter with my cat, looking like he belonged there. "Did I hurt you earlier?"

The little I did know about rough, tough cowboys is they would never admit anyone inflicted pain, but especially not a girl.

"Of course not," he said, although his hand absently rubbed across his stomach.

"I could be completely off base, but I bet you'll have a bruise."

"I don't make bets and it's fine," he said, continuing to pet Hemi. The cat's purrs grew louder, if that was possible.

Guilt over assaulting Tim, again, settled over me. As a peace offering, I held up the last bite of fudge. "This is an exception to the rule, because I don't share my chocolate, but I'll give you a bite."

"Nah. You eat it. Aunt Charli made so many treats, I need to start avoiding them or I'll end up with a belly like Santa Claus before New Year's."

That comment almost made me snort in disbelief. From what I'd seen, Tim was a long, long way from having to worry about a pot belly. How much fudge would it take to turn a virile young man with washboard abs into a jolly old elf? More than Charli had made, I'm sure.

I popped the last bite in my mouth and wiped my hands on a tissue I pulled from a box I kept on the counter.

Tim set Hemi down and moved in front of me so swiftly, his lips were pressed to mine before I knew what was happening.

Not that I minded.

My arms snaked around his neck and I returned his kiss. For the length of several racing heartbeats, he held me in his arms and kissed me more passionately than I'd ever been kissed in my life.

When he pulled back, he wore that lopsided grin I was quickly coming to adore. He licked his lips as a devilish light twinkled in his amazing eyes. "Mmm. I think that was the best tasting chocolate I've ever had."

A blush warmed my cheeks and I started to step back, but the circle of his arms kept me from retreating.

"Don't run off, Carol. Not yet."

I turned my head and pressed my cheek against his chest. His heart pounded beneath my ear, matching the accelerated rhythm of mine. He smelled so good and felt so solid and safe, I wanted to stay there the rest of the day.

Unfortunately, that wasn't an option.

Hemi jumped onto the counter and meowed, reminding me the entire world had not disappeared just because Tim Burke was holding me in his strong arms.

"I better get on over to the feed store. Miles will give me a bad time as it is." Tim picked up his hat that at some point in the last few minutes had landed on the floor. He dusted off the brim then settled it on his head, took my hand in his and kissed my fingers as we walked to the door.

At least he walked to the door. The minute his lips touched the back of my hand, my legs had all the strength of soggy noodles. I had no idea how they carried me across the store.

"I'll talk to you later, Christmas Carol. Thanks for having breakfast with me." He pecked my cheek and disappeared out the door.

It took five minutes before I regained the ability to move and think simultaneously. What was I doing letting Tim Burke take me to breakfast and kiss me and completely turn my head?

Nothing good could come of it.

# *Chapter Seven*

Karen walked over to where I set out Victorian-replica snow globes next to a selection of leather-bound Charles Dickens books.

"I had an idea," she said, reaching for a box and carefully removing a snow globe with a pair of skaters nestled inside the sparkly liquid.

I watched as she slowly turned the globe upside down, then right side up. Iridescent shards of glitter floated around the couple. "What's your idea?"

In what probably seemed like a lifetime ago to her, Karen had a job for a marketing company in Seattle. Then she met the man who'd become her husband and moved to Montana to be a stay-at-home mother to two adorable little terrors. Karen was incredibly good at coming up with promotional ideas and marketing plans. I'd learned to pay attention whenever she had an idea to share.

"We need a Santa."

"A Santa or *the* Santa?" I teased. "I've heard the jolly old elf can be hard to pin down this time of year."

She set the snow globe on the shelf with the others. "We need someone to pretend to be Santa Claus. I think it would be a great idea if we did a story time with Santa event, preferably this Saturday. We could give each child that attends a candy cane and…"

"Fabulous idea," I said, beaming at her. This is why I put up with her two hooligans when her mother-in-law drops them off at the store on her way to knitting club. Those two boys are like a demolition team, bent on destroying everything in their path. Honestly, I don't know how Karen handles them, even if they are as cute as can be.

"If we can find a Santa today and set a time for Saturday, we could get the word out around town," Karen hastened to explain. "I thought it would be something fun and would be a nice community thing for the store to do."

"I agree and I know someone who'd make a great Santa." I took my phone from my pocket and hesitated before I called Aspen Grove Ranch. This was probably not a message to leave with Nancy to pass on to Tim. If I wanted him to be our Santa, I should probably ask him directly because Nancy wouldn't give him the option of refusing.

"You aren't going to call Miles Wilson, are you? His scowls would frighten the kids half to death."

I shook my head. "No, I'm not going to call Miles. I'm not calling anyone, but I am sending a text to our potential Saint Nick."

Karen tossed me a knowing look as she set another snow globe on the shelf. "If the Santa in question is that hunky cowboy you've been keeping company with recently, by all means, ask him."

My eyebrows shot upward. "I have not been keeping company with anyone. He's Nancy Wright's grandson, as I believe you well know."

"I do know that. I also know your eyes sparkle with excitement when anyone mentions Aspen Grove Ranch or Nancy, and you positively glow when that cowboy swaggers in here."

"There is no sparkling or glowing happening. None at all."

Karen laughed. "Whatever you say, girl, but I'm telling you, that man has tickled your fancy."

*Tickled my fancy?* Hah! Karen couldn't be more off base. I hardly gave Tim Burke a passing thought, unless you counted thinking about his dreamy smile, those gorgeous eyes, or the deep sound of his voice dozens of times a day as having your fancy tickled.

Before I could change my mind, I tapped out a message to Tim and sent it.

*I hate to impose, but would you possibly have time to help me with something Saturday morning for a few hours?*

I shoved my phone back in my pocket,

expecting to wait hours for a reply from him, but my phone chimed a few minutes later.

*Whatever you need, Carol, I'm happy to help. When and where?*

Despite my first impression of him, Tim truly was a wonderful guy. He hadn't even asked for particulars before he offered his assistance. To me, that was what a true friend did. Jumped in to help with no questions asked. I knew Tim was busy and wasn't overly fond of coming to town, so it meant even more to me that he'd readily volunteer his time.

*Here at the store. If you could arrive around 9:30 that would be perfect. Do you need specifics?*

His last message made me smile.

*Nope. See you Saturday, Christmas Carol.*

It wasn't just that he called me Christmas Carol, but that he'd included a Christmas tree and heart emoji. Lest I obsess over what he meant by sending the heart, I instead informed Karen we had a Santa.

"Yes!" she said, giving me a high-five. "I bet if you wanted to make a small fortune for the toys and clothes funds for the kids, you could have him wear only a pair of snug jeans, his cowboy boots, and Santa hat. If you sold tickets for ten bucks each to let big girls sit on his lap and have their picture taken, you'd have more takers than you could handle."

It was a good thing I wasn't taking a sip of tea then because I would have choked on it. "Karen!"

She just laughed and hurried off to help a customer.

The rest of the day, the image she created was stuck in my mind. Rather than focus on it, I tried to keep busy. When Josie arrived, I told her about story time with Santa and she volunteered to be the elf. While she was excitedly explaining in detail a costume she could borrow from school, I watched the purple-haired girl come into the store and make a beeline for the alcove at the back.

Since the first day I'd spoken to her, I'd made a little headway in finding out more about her. Josie told me her name was Mia McBride and she was a freshman. I'd made inquiries with my friends to see if any of them knew about her family, but no one had any info, other than the drunk who owned the garage in town was named McBride.

It seemed too much of a coincidence to ignore. I wanted to help the girl who was obviously struggling through a rough patch, but I had no idea what to do. Memories of how Mr. Abernathy had earned my trust surfaced.

In my campaign to befriend Mia, I began leaving an after-school snack for her in the alcove. The first day it remained untouched, but the past few days, she'd either eaten it or stuffed it in her backpack.

The store was busy, so an hour went by before I made my way back to her spot behind the used book section. She had school books spread around her as she sat cross-legged on the pillows in the alcove and was munching on the peanut-butter filled celery sticks I'd left for her. Feeling quite creative, I'd added halved pretzels at the top of the celery stick for antlers, a raspberry at the bottom for a nose, and chocolate chips for eyes.

From the way Mia smiled as she picked up another one and looked at it before taking a bite, she appreciated the treat.

Rather than interrupt her, I backed away and returned to the front of the store. Josie and I talked about story time with Santa in between stocking shelves, cleaning, and waiting on customers.

It was just a few minutes before closing time when I saw Mia looking at the display of snow globes Karen and I had set out earlier.

"They play music," I said, stepping behind her.

She gasped and almost dropped the snow globe she held. A look of terror settled on her face as she returned it to the shelf and spun away from me, intent on making a quick escape out the door.

"Mia, it's okay. Nothing is broken, besides, I shouldn't have startled you." I wanted to give the poor girl a hug in the worst way, but had an idea she wouldn't welcome it. Not now.

"Night, Carol! See you tomorrow," Josie called as she turned the open sign to closed and left for the evening.

"Are you in a hurry, Mia?" I asked.

"I should probably get home," she said, although she didn't make a move like she planned to leave.

"Do you like tea?" I asked, uncertain what to do to build her trust.

She shrugged, but watched as I turned the lock on the door then motioned for her to follow me to the little room my employees used for breaks. There was a microwave, a refrigerator, a table with four chairs, and a tiny counter where I kept baskets of granola bars, individually packaged crackers, and a bowl of whole fruit.

"Help yourself," I said, motioning to the counter as I filled two mugs with water from the hot tap installed on the edge of the sink and added tea bags.

Mia seemed hesitant, but she walked over to the counter and chose a bright red apple, tucking it inside her backpack.

I added a spoon of sugar to each mug and set them both on the table.

Mia took a seat across the table from me and sipped her tea. "It tastes like Christmas," she said, chancing a glance at me before taking another sip.

"It's called Paris Holiday," I said, enjoying a drink of the sweet tea. Chocolate and a hint of lavender blended with peppermint for a tea that was perfect with dessert, or anytime, in my humble opinion.

"I like it," Mia said, taking another long drink.

Rather than ask Mia even one of the many questions skittering through my thoughts, I leaned back and smiled at her. "You know, when I was your age, I used to come to this store to hide out from my mom. She never thought to look for me here and Mr. Abernathy, he was the owner then, let me read the used books back in the alcove. It was my spot for many years. Eventually, when I was old enough, he hired me to work in the store part-time. I bought the store a year ago when I moved back to Christmas Mountain."

The girl didn't say anything, but she pushed a lock of hair out of her eyes and gave me a cautious glance.

"If it wasn't for this store, for the refuge I found here when I most needed it, I'm not sure how I would have survived my childhood."

Mia's gaze met mine and I could see the pain there. Pain and fear, and a sadness that went all the way down to her soul. I wanted to give her comfort and hope, but wasn't sure she was ready for either.

"I just wanted you to know, Mia, that you are always welcome in the store. And if you ever need anything, need someone to talk to who understands, or help with anything, I hope you'll let me know."

Slowly, she nodded, but continued drinking her tea instead of speaking. When the mug was empty, she got up and washed it, returning it to the cupboard where I'd taken it from.

"Thank you, Miss Bennett. I better go now."

"Of course," I said, walking with her to the door. "Do you need a ride home?"

"No. My brother will drive me home. He's not far from here." She stepped outside and gave me a wave before she hurried up the street.

Well, at least I knew she had a brother who cared enough to give her a ride.

Heart heavy with worry over the girl, I did my evening bookwork, cleaned the store, then called

Joy after I was sure Max would be in bed.

"Hey, Carol," Joy said in a cheerful voice as she answered the phone.

"It sounds like you had a good day," I said, trying not to leap right into what was bothering me.

"I did have a good day."

"Run into any cute guys today?" I asked, unable to stop myself from teasing her a bit.

"Just never mind. What's up with you? You sound worried."

Joy had always been perceptive of my moods.

"I am worried." After I told her about Mia and my concerns, Joy offered me good advice. By the time we hung up, I felt much better, but determined to keep an eye out for the girl.

## *Chapter Eight*

Whether it was the enthusiasm of my employees, the flyers Karen made, or the way word of something out of the ordinary spreads like wildfire through a small town that drew a crowd to my store for story time with Santa, something had worked.

Parents with children in tow began arriving shortly after I opened my doors. I was glad Karen had agreed to come in and help during the event because I needed every able body I could get.

My friend Cassandra came with her sweet little boy, Dusty, who was four. And Joy arrived with Max. Although I was sure Max thought he was far too old to listen to Santa read at the ripe old age of seven, he seemed happy to run around the store with the other youngsters.

Children raced up and down the stairs, trying to figure out a way to jump onto Rudolph as he hung above the cash register. I heard puzzle pieces being scattered across the floor and a crash when one of the snow globes was knocked off the shelf.

"I didn't know this many kids existed in the whole county," I commented to Karen as we cleaned up the broken snow globe and wiped the liquid off the floor. My hardwoods would be embedded with glitter for months.

She laughed and gave me a pat on the shoulder. "Just be glad my husband is keeping the boys entertained at home this morning."

"I'm wildly grateful Peter took one for the team," I teased. "Tell him he has my undying gratitude."

The bell above the door jangled and Karen nudged me in the ribs so hard, I almost dropped the pieces of snow globe I held in a dustpan. I looked up to see Tim standing just inside the door, gazing around the store with a hefty dose of apprehension.

If the guy turned around and left, I wouldn't have blamed him. I was pretty sure the store looked like someone had turned a cage full of monkeys loose.

"Go get your fella," Karen said, taking the dustpan from my hand and giving me a shove forward.

"He's not mine," I hissed under my breath then pasted on a carefree smile and hurried to Tim before he made an escape outside.

"Hey, stranger!" My voice sounded fake and

far too upbeat as I looped my arm around his and pulled him down the hallway toward the storage room.

"What's going on?" he asked as the noise receded behind us when I shut the storage room door. Poor Hemi had retreated to his bed and most likely wouldn't stick a whisker out of the room until closing time.

Tim hunkered down and the cat trotted over to him. If he could have talked, Hemi probably would have tattled that Tim was about to get very involved in the chaos erupting in the store. The cat rolled onto his back, motor running at top speed while Tim scratched his belly. I tried to decide how best to broach the topic at hand.

When Tim didn't want specifics about what I had planned today, I took that as a perfect excuse not to have to beg and plead with him to be Santa. Now, I realized being upfront with him about my plans would have been the smart thing to do.

After he said he'd help me, I'd ordered a Santa suit I was sure would fit his broad frame and had it express shipped. There was a big red velvet sack stuffed full of inexpensive paperback books, all gift-wrapped (which had taken me until midnight to finish last night). Each child who came would get a candy cane, but I decided to have Josie pass those out at the door as the kids were leaving. The last thing that wild bunch of youngsters needed was sugar this morning. Visions of candy-smeared books danced in my head, confirming the wisdom of giving them the treat as they left my store.

Tim looked up at me and smiled. Warmth

blazed in his eyes and I found myself wishing I could just ask him for a hug instead of preparing to beseech him to put on a bright red suit.

"So, what can I help you with today, Christmas Carol?" he asked in a lighthearted tone I was sure was about to disappear. By the time this was all said and done, Tim might never speak to me again and I didn't like the thought of that. Not at all.

"Did you really mean it when you said you'd help with anything?"

"Of course." He stood and settled his hands on my arms, searching my face. "What's wrong? Did something happen?"

"I'm fine, Tim, but thank you. What I need your help with today is... well, you see... um..."

"Just spit it out, Carol." There was that lopsided grin, guaranteed to make my knees turn to a wobbly mass akin to gelatin.

"I need you to be Santa for the kids for story time and the suit is hanging right there and it starts in twenty minutes and I have the books and a chair all ready for you." The words rolled out of me so fast, I sounded like someone had pressed the fast-forward button.

To his credit, Tim didn't march out the back door, which is what I probably would have done if I was in his boots. However, he did drop his hands from my arms, take a long step back, and glower at me. He removed his hat, raked a hand over his head, then scrubbed it over his face.

"Say that again, slower."

"I should have mentioned it earlier, but what I need you to help me with today is story time with

Santa. Karen came up with the idea and it was clearly a good one. I ordered a Santa suit that should fit you well. The kids are expecting Santa to arrive at ten."

Tim glanced at his watch, released a sigh that must have come all the way from the soles of his boots, and shrugged out of his coat.

"What do you need me to do?" he asked as I handed him the pants. He toed off his boots and pulled the velvet pants on over his jeans. The fabric bagged and sagged in the seat, were tight in the thighs, but would serve the purpose.

"I have a chair all set up where the children will gather around you. They'll sit on the floor. There are five storybooks next to the chair. You don't have to read all of them, but if you could end with *Twas the Night Before Christmas,* that would be wonderful. It's a cowboy version, instead of the standard story."

"And that's it? Read a few stories and toss out a few ho-ho-hos?"

"Basically. We did not advertise photos with Santa. It's up to you if you want to let parents snap photos of the kids on your lap."

I caught his eye roll as he tried to get the Santa coat on over his heavy flannel shirt. The shoulders were so tight, he could barely move.

"I don't think it's going to fit," I said, wondering how air deprived lungs have to be before a person passes out from lack of oxygen. At the moment, I couldn't seem to remember how to breathe. If he couldn't get into the Santa outfit, I was going to have a store full of protesting parents and unhappy, disappointed children.

Tim worked the coat off and gave a tug on his shirt. Snaps popped open right along with my mouth. I wished I could have written a personal thank-you note to the person who invented western shirts. He took off his shirt and I could do nothing but stare at the thin, white undershirt covering his sculpted chest. Karen was right. Women would line up all the way to the Sugar Plum Inn for a chance to sit on Tim's lap and have their photo taken, especially if he wasn't wearing the Santa coat.

Vaguely aware of him trying to figure out how to put on the padding, the snap of his fingers in my face drew me out of mindlessly ogling his impressive form.

"How do I get this thing on?" he asked, holding out the padded belly.

"I think it goes like this." I stepped behind him, sliding straps over his shoulders, then tying strings in the back. Only by sheer determination to stay focused did I manage to keep my fingers on task instead of trailing over his muscles.

I grabbed the coat and held it while he shoved his arms in the sleeves. It was still a tight fit in the shoulders, but he could at least move his arms now. The belly part of the coat had plenty of room.

He picked up the belt and fastened it around his waist then glanced around. "Beard?"

I handed it to him and watched as he put it and the wig on. He noticed a small mirror hanging on the wall and went over to it, adjusting the left side of the beard where it drooped.

With a glance over his shoulder at me, he

asked. "Where is the Santa hat?"

"I thought you might prefer to wear your hat and boots."

"My boots, your hat," he said and stamped his feet into his boots.

I lifted the Santa hat and settled it on the wig at a jaunty angle then stepped back. Not bad. I walked in a circle around him. Not bad at all.

"You look perfect, Tim. I can't thank you enough for…"

His fingers on my lips effectively silenced me. "We'll talk about this later."

Dread caused a tight knot to form in my stomach as I handed him a pair of white gloves then gave him the sack full of books.

"Each child gets a book from Santa. Since they are wrapped, they can't fight over who gets what."

He nodded, inhaled a deep breath, and motioned for me to precede him into the store.

I squared my shoulders, marched down the hall, and went to stand in front of the big wingback chair Aiden and I had carried near the front of the store from one of the cozy reading nooks.

"Thank you all for coming today," I said in my loudest voice. When children continued running and yelling, I whistled just like my dad had taught me. Apparently, no one expected the shrill burst of sound because silence fell over the entire store in the next breath. "Thank you for being here today. If the children will sit around this chair, Santa will be here in just a minute."

Josie, dressed in her green elf outfit with red and white striped tights, skipped over to the chair and the children followed her like she was the Pied Piper.

"What do you think would make Santa come faster?" I asked, hoping Tim picked up on my cues. "Should we sing a song for him?"

"Yes!" the kids shouted.

I started singing "Here Comes Santa Claus." Karen, bless her heart, picked up a jingle bell from the Christmas display and began ringing it.

A loud, deep ho-ho-ho floated over the store and the children, as one, turned to watch Santa suddenly appear.

Tim could have been a professional Santa actor as he portrayed the jolly old elf. Good sport that he was, he read all five books then spent another hour letting children climb on his lap while parents snapped photos. Some of the kids screamed, two rotten boys kicked his shins, and one little rascal yanked so hard on his beard, it snapped back up and caught Tim on the nose. I winced because I knew it had to hurt.

Mindful that Nancy would have wanted to see Tim in action, I did take a short video and texted it to her. She'd immediately called, laughing so hard I could hardly understand her. Around her giggles, I got the idea she thought roping him into being Santa was one of the funniest things she'd ever seen.

Tim smiled and tossed around ho-ho-hos as though it was Christmas confetti. I had no idea he was so good with kids and the part of me that someday wanted to have my own family sat up and took notice. I could practically feel my biological clock ticking away as I watched him hug a shy little girl with her hair in pigtails and shiny red shoes on her feet.

If I was looking for someone special and had a list of qualifications, Tim would have checked all the boxes. Every last one of them. But I wasn't looking and that was all there was to it.

As the last child climbed off his lap and took her mother's hand, Tim motioned to me. I hurried over, ready to do whatever it took to earn his forgiveness for springing this on him.

"Well, Carol, have you been a good girl this year?" he asked in his deep voice.

The obvious answer to that question would have been a resounding "no" since I'd coerced him into being Santa under questionable pretenses.

When I didn't immediately respond, he pulled me onto his lap and nuzzled my neck with his synthetic beard.

Of course, my employees started to laugh and Karen hurried over, snapping photos with her phone. The big hand splayed across my middle and the arm of steel attached to it kept me from leaping up and cowering behind the cash register.

"Santa wants a photo of this naughty girl to go in the naughty and nice book." Tim handed Karen the phone he'd somehow dug out of his pocket.

She laughed and snapped a few images then returned the phone to him.

"Santa said she's naughty, Mom. Will he put coal in her stocking?" Dusty asked as Cassandra led him out of the store with a quick wave in my direction and a motion with her hand that she wanted me to call her later. No doubt, she'd want to hear all about where I found Santa and why I was trapped on his lap.

"You owe me big time," Tim whispered under his breath as he released me and I hopped off his lap with as much dignity as I could muster. He stood, gave a grand wave to those who were still in the store, and disappeared down the hallway to the storage room. I waited five minutes, then made my way back there. He was just tugging on his boots when I stuck my head around the door. I felt a twinge of disappointment I'd missed seeing him with just the thin undershirt hiding all that muscle.

"Tim, listen, I'm sorry. I should have..." Fingers pressed to my lips silenced me again. The feel of them there was thoroughly unnerving, but I sure wasn't going to push them away.

"Tomorrow afternoon you'll come out to the ranch and you can grovel then. Fair enough?"

I nodded. "What time should I be there?"

"Do you want to come for lunch?" he asked as he pulled on his coat and settled his hat on his head.

I did, but I didn't feel I deserved one of Charli's excellent meals. "No, but I could be there about one, if that works for you."

"I'll see you then. Wear clothes you aren't afraid to get dirty and I mean really, really dirty. Dress warm and wear boots." He gave Hemi one last scratch behind his ears, tipped his hat to me, and left via the back door without another word.

I locked the door and picked up the cat. "I think I really stepped in it this time, kitty."

Hemi's purrs sounded more like "I told you so," as I set him on his bed and went back to work.

## Chapter Nine

Once, when I was about seven, I ransacked my mom's wallet, took all the cash, and went on a spending spree in Christmas Mountain while she was locked in her home office, trying to meet a deadline. I bought a new outfit, a bag full of toys, and stuffed myself so full of ice cream, cookies, and soda, it made me sick. To this day, I can't stand the taste of Mountain Dew.

Anyway, when I got home, Mom was ready to hang me from the rafters by my toenails. Only she didn't have time. Instead, she made me sit in a room that was only used when she declared I needed a time-out session and told me she'd deal with me when she finished her work. Honestly, I think it was supposed to be a storage closet. No windows, no throw rugs, no pictures on the wall. Nada. Nothing. Just beige walls, a straight back chair, and a bare light bulb.

So I sat in that room, tummy gurgling from an overload of sweets and dread of what punishment she'd mete out later. I came up with a hundred different ways my mother could pour more wretchedness into my life as I waited and waited and waited. At the time, I was sure I spent weeks in there, but it was probably closer to a few hours. When Dad came home, he found me sitting on that chair, tears running down my cheeks. He gave me a hug and sent me to my room then went to talk to Mom.

I never did receive additional punishment for my transgressions. I finally figured out the misery of waiting was the punishment.

And darn if that Tim Burke hadn't done the same thing to me.

I'd been tied in knots since he left the store yesterday. It wasn't that I minded doing whatever chores he thought would atone for my actions. But the uncertainty was about to kill me.

After I got home from church and ate a quick lunch of a toasted cheese sandwich, I dug through my clothes until I extracted my oldest, most worn pair of jeans. I figured they had enough life in them for one or two more washings, but that was about it. The seams inside were frayed and a spot just below the rear left pocket would be threadbare soon.

I dressed in a set of thermal underwear before I slid into the jeans. I added a turtleneck that had seen better days, then topped it with a sweatshirt that

123

proclaimed I was a Montana State University fan when I'd always preferred the University of Montana (not that I actually went to any college). After pulling on a pair of thick wool socks, I got down on my hands and knees to dig into the very back of the closet to unearth a pair of cowboy boots I used to wear when I'd go with Dad to visit a friend who'd let us ride horses on his place.

A coat with a huge coffee stain on the front (not mine, but a result of someone walking and texting then blindly running into me) would keep me warm and I wouldn't have to be concerned about it getting dirty.

A thick scarf, a pair of fleece lined gloves, and a stocking cap completed my outerwear selections. Quickly braiding my long hair, I fastened the end with a rubber band, snagged my purse, and headed off to face my punishment.

The drive from town to Aspen Grove Ranch was lovely. Sun glistened on the snow and sparkled like diamonds in the afternoon light. Yet, the anxiety of facing Tim and whatever chores he had planned for me sent my anxiety into orbit. The cheese sandwich rested in my stomach like a rock and I wished I'd skipped eating anything. I should have had a cup of soothing mint tea, or maybe some chamomile.

I tried to think of anything except whatever awaited me at the ranch. Even singing my favorite holiday tunes couldn't draw my thoughts from what awaited me at Aspen Grove.

When I parked in front of the house, Brutus ran out to greet me. I expected him to be standoffish, or at least growl, but he must have remembered me from Thanksgiving. The friendly canine licked my hand and practically beat a hole in my front fender wagging his tail against it.

Tim stepped out onto the front porch and waved so I headed his way.

"You're right on time," he said, not smiling, not kissing my cheek or touching my hand. He stepped back so I could enter the house. "Nana and Aunt Charli are in by the fire. I thought you might want to pop in and say hello then we'll head out. While you do that, I'll get my coat."

I nodded and set my purse on a bench by the door then walked into the great room. Nancy sat in what had to be her favorite chair while Charli lounged on the couch with a magazine open on her lap.

"Hello, Carol! How are you?" Nancy offered me a welcoming smile and motioned me to come closer.

"I'm well. How are you both doing?"

Charli grinned. "I'm fantastic and Nancy is getting better every day, even if she gripes too much."

Nancy stuck out her tongue at her sister, then grabbed my hand. "I don't know how you talked Tim into playing Santa but that was the best thing I've seen in ages, maybe ever."

Charli nodded. "I couldn't believe you got him in a Santa suit, especially with all those kids. How did you do it?"

"I asked him if he had time to help me with a special project. He said he did. Then I asked if he wanted any specifics and he said he trusted me." I shrugged. "But I get the idea I'm in big trouble with him."

"Oh, big, big trouble," Nancy said, although her eyes twinkled with mirth. She glanced at my stained coat, worn jeans, and scuffed boots. "Did he tell you he was going to put you to work this afternoon?"

"No, but he said to wear old clothes I don't mind getting really, really dirty and to dress warm."

"I have no idea what that boy has planned, but don't let him give you any grief," Nancy said, squeezing my fingers.

"When you come back in, we'll have tea. I love that Christmas tea you brought to Nancy," Charli said. "I hope you'll stay for dinner. I'm making pecan-crusted chicken with parmesan potatoes."

"As delicious as that sounds, I should probably wait to see how this afternoon goes with Tim before I impose my presence upon you for dinner."

"I heard my name," Tim said, walking into the room dressed in the same chore coat he'd worn the last time I was at the ranch. He had an old cowboy hat on his head and held a pair of gloves in his hand. He stared at me. "Ready to get at it?"

"Sure," I said, forcing myself to sound cheerful and smile.

"You'll be fine," Nancy whispered before she let go of my hand. "And you're staying for dinner."

I followed Tim outside. As we walked toward the barn, I yanked the stocking cap over my head, pulled on my gloves, and resolved myself to face whatever it was with a smile on my face.

Fully expecting to have a shovel thrust into my hand and left to muck out stalls for the afternoon, I was shocked when Tim opened the barn door and led out two horses, already saddled.

"Thought you might like to go for a ride."

"I'd love to!" Okay, I've always had a thing for horses and the opportunities for me to ride are few and far between. It's hard to curb the enthusiasm when you truly are giddy with excitement.

He grinned. "This is Jude. Nana used to ride her all the time before her hip started bothering her. She's a nice, gentle horse."

The buckskin mare had the sweetest face and I was immediately in love. With the horse. Not the cowboy.

"I think we'll get along fine," I said, taking the reins Tim handed to me.

"Have you ridden before?"

I nodded. "It's been a while, though."

"It will all come back to you."

Before he could offer to help me on Jude, I set my foot in the stirrup and swung into the saddle. His hand on my thigh made me look down my nose at him with a scowl until I realized he was trying to adjust the stirrup so it fit my long legs.

"Thank you," I said as he finished the left one and moved around to the other side.

"Feel okay?" he asked, glancing up at me.

"Yes. At least from what I remember, I think it's about the right length."

He swung onto the back of Rowan, his big bay horse, and led the way away from the buildings and out across an empty field.

I wanted to ask where we were headed, what work he wanted me to do, what punishment he had planned for the whole Santa thing. Instead, I kept my mouth shut and enjoyed the ride and the beautiful winter day.

We'd ridden about half an hour when we neared a grouping of towering fir trees. Beneath the shelter of their thick branches the ground was bare, except for pinecones and needles. Tim stopped and stepped out of the saddle. I reined in near him, not surprised that my backside was starting to go numb and my thighs ached. At least I was relatively warm with all my layers of clothes, though.

When I stepped out of the stirrup, I leaned against Jude for a minute until my legs felt a little steadier.

Tim removed a Pendleton wool blanket he'd tied behind his saddle and pulled something out of his saddlebags. Amazed, I watched as he spread a blanket on the ground then set what appeared to be a thermos on one corner, along with a thick manila envelope.

"Come on, you troublesome girl, and sit here with me for a while." He held his hand out to me.

Confused, I just stared at him. "What happened to me mucking out stalls or shoveling manure in the feedlot, or something equally as unpleasant?"

He chuckled. "I never said I expected you to do any of those things. I just let you think you were going to be doing something awful as payback, which was the payback, or at least most of it."

"I knew it!" I crowed, then took his hand and walked with him to the blanket. We sat down, not too close, and he opened the thermos, poured liquid into the cup, and handed it to me.

I sniffed and took a sip of the hot chocolate. It was perfect. Not too hot, not too sweet, with just a hint of peppermint. "Mmm. Did Charli make this?"

"She might have offered a bit of instruction," he said, guiding my hand to his mouth so he could take a drink. "It's pretty good if I do say so myself."

He leaned back on his elbows and gazed out at the ranch.

Mesmerized by the view (and I didn't mean just Tim), I could have remained there for hours watching clouds float across the sky or the deer on the other side of the pasture as they hid in the trees. I'd already discovered Tim made a wonderful companion. And the more time I spent with him, the more at ease I felt with him.

Content, I sighed. "It's wonderful out here, Tim. So peaceful and lovely. You are blessed to live in such a beautiful place."

"I am," he said, taking another sip of the chocolate when I held the cup out to him.

"I really do apologize for yesterday. I had no idea that many kids would show up and I do feel bad about springing the Santa suit surprise on you out of the blue. I promise I won't ever do anything like that again." And I wouldn't. Tim's friendship had come to mean a great deal to me and I wouldn't knowingly do anything to jeopardize it.

He raised an eyebrow but didn't say anything. We sat in silence for a while, then Tim gave me a long, studying glance.

"I do think you owe me a little something after

yesterday."

I wondered what he had in mind. Kisses were a payment I was more than happy to deliver. "Such as?" I asked, my gaze focused on his enticing mouth.

Heat blazed in his eyes, but he smirked. "I think you should have to answer a question for every kid that sat on my lap."

Good heavens! It seemed to me there were a hundred kids in the store. I had no intention of revealing that much about my life to him. Not a single doubt existed in my mind that his questions wouldn't be about a new bestseller or the weather.

"I'll answer ten questions."

A frown creased his forehead and he sat forward, placing his elbows on bent knees as he stared at me. Eventually, he nodded in agreement. I assumed he had a long list of questions prepared, but he appeared to be considering what to ask first.

"What's one of your favorite memories of your dad?"

The question caught me completely off guard. I'd expected an interrogation about why I moved back to Christmas Mountain or where I was all the years between leaving and buying the bookstore since that is a secret I didn't readily share.

Instead of thinking about what I didn't want to answer, I considered Tim's question. I had so many wonderful memories of my dad, it wasn't easy to choose one.

"My mom wasn't one to get into the holidays, but Dad always did his best to make it special. The year I was fifteen, my mom flew to Los Angeles to meet with a client in December. She was gone almost two weeks. Dad and I decked the halls until it looked like one of Santa's elves was having a rummage sale. We sang carols, attended all the community events, and we even went ice skating at a pond Dad had found a few miles out of town. I helped him cut down a tree and we decorated it. And we executed a very poor attempt at making fudge." I grinned at him. "But we ate it anyway. It was pretty good spooned over ice cream."

He smiled. "It sounds like your father was a really good man and a great dad."

"He was. I miss him every day." Mindful to keep things light, I quirked an eyebrow and looked at Tim. "Nine more left. What's the next question?"

"If you could live anywhere in the world, where would you choose?"

"Christmas Mountain." I answered without thinking because it was the truth. I loved living in the community where I grew up. "I've been to a lot of places and none of them compare to here. It's home."

Evidently, whatever I said pleased him because his face practically beamed with joy.

He leaned back on his elbows again and stretched out those long, muscular legs. "Of all the places you've visited, pick your top three and tell me why you chose them."

Thought and consideration were required to answer this question. I'd traveled all over the world and seen so many incredible things. It was hard to pick only three, but I finally narrowed down the list.

I took another sip of the rapidly cooling

chocolate then held the cup out to Tim. He took the last drink then refilled it, handing it back to me. I wrapped my hands around the cup, grateful for the warmth. Sitting on the ground, even if it was on a beautiful Native American inspired blanket, in the shade of the trees on a chilly December day isn't a great way to stay warm.

I glanced at Tim and took another sip of the chocolate before I answered his question.

"If I had to pick just three places, which is super hard, the top three, in no particular order would be Lake Bled in Slovenia, Castelluccio in Italy, and Smith Rock in Oregon."

Although he didn't say anything, from the befuddled expression on his face, I was sure he expected me to rattle off big cities like New York, Tokyo, and Paris.

"Why?" he asked, taking the chocolate from my hand and drinking deeply before he gave it back to me.

"Have you ever heard of Lake Bled?" At the shake of his head, I continued. "The town is less than ten thousand in population, but there's a magnificent emerald green lake with a tiny island in the middle with a church built right on its cliff. There's a castle built in the eleventh century clinging to the slopes and it's surrounded on all sides by towering mountains topped with snow and covered by ancient forests. You expect dragons and knights to appear at any moment."

"And for a girl who loves books, was it like stepping into a fairytale?" Tim asked with a grin.

"It definitely was. It's a place I hope to visit

again someday."

"How about the place in Italy? Would you go back there?"

"Yes, in June. Castelluccio is a tiny little village located on a hill in the midst of a sprawling plateau. From there, the view is spectacular, divided into three plains. Every year, between the end of May and July, those plains explode with color as thousands and thousands of flowers bloom. It literally looks like someone took an artist's palette and spilled it over the earth."

"Wow!" Tim looked wistful, like he longed to see it for himself. He turned to me and raised an eyebrow in question. "And Smith Rock? After those two locales, you have to explain why a place in Oregon makes your list."

I shrugged. "Smith Rock is a state park in Central Oregon's high desert region. I think it's about six hundred acres or so. The rocks there are welded tuff, formed eons ago by compressed volcanic ash. And the Crooked River flows through it. Sunset or sunrise are just mind-boggling in their beauty. I loved hiking there. My dad and I went there for a week the summer I was thirteen and had the best time."

Tim remained silent for a while. I wondered what thoughts tumbled through his handsome head when he finally looked over at me. "What made you hide from your mom at the bookstore, Carol? What drove you there?"

"Well, I tried hiding at the library or at my friends' homes, but she found me." I wanted to be flippant, but he was having no part of it as he continued staring at me, waiting for the truth. Might as well just rip off that Band-Aid and be done with it. "From the time I was a toddler until I left home, my mother had my entire future planned out in minute detail. The problem was she never stopped to ask me what I wanted. Every day after school she'd drag me from one thing to another until I just couldn't take it anymore. No amount of pleading from me or even my dad putting his foot down would change her mind. But if she couldn't find me, she couldn't have her way. Of course, when the bookstore closed and I had to go home, things never went well, but Dad was there to serve as a buffer."

His hand settled on mine and he gave it a comforting squeeze. "I'm sorry, Carol. It sounds like you had a miserable childhood."

"No, not miserable. The time I spent with my dad was amazing. I just wish I'd had more time with him before he passed away." Grief and regret formed a lump in my throat that I worked to swallow along with another sip of chocolate.

He must have sensed my struggle because the next question brought me back to an even keel. "What's the worst thing you've ever tasted?"

"Durian."

His nose wrinkled. "Oh, man, those are just nasty. A buddy dared me to try one. The smell was enough to knock me out of my boots and it didn't taste any better."

I laughed. "When my a… friend cut one open and told me to try it, my eyes started watering from the smell. I took one bite and spit it into the garbage. It was so bad."

"Agreed," he said, taking the chocolate from me and emptying the cup then setting it back on the thermos. "What's the best thing you've ever eaten?"

I tossed him a saucy grin. "Anything made by your Aunt Charli. Seriously, she is amazing. I ate at Magdala a few times when I was in Chicago. Because the meals were so delicious, I can't help but wonder if she was the one who prepared them."

"If she didn't, she was probably overseeing the chef that did."

We'd been outside a while now and the longer we sat, the more the cold seeped into me. In spite of my efforts to fight it off, I shivered.

"Chilly?" Tim asked, but before I could respond, he scooted behind me, wrapped his arms around my waist, and pulled me back against his chest. Suddenly, I felt quite tropical. Heat poured over me, around me, surrounding me in a kind of warmth I'd never known, never dreamed existed. And I really didn't want it to end.

I relaxed and leaned back with my head nestled against his shoulder. If I turned my head a few inches, it would be so easy to kiss those luscious lips of his.

"Favorite movie?"

Nothing like a string of questions to interrupt any amorous thoughts I might have entertained.

"Angel and the Badman with…"

"John Wayne," Tim said before I could finish my sentence. "I didn't peg you for an old westerns fan."

"Then you have indeed pegged me erroneously, Mr. Burke." I gave him a haughty look then softened it with a grin. "My dad loved John Wayne and we'd watch those old movies whenever Mom wasn't around. And before you ask, I love country music, good barbecue, and know the difference between straw and hay."

"Now I'm impressed," he said gently, tightening his grip around me. I wasn't certain if he truly was impressed or just said that, but then again, Tim didn't seem to have any trouble holding back his thoughts or opinions. "What's your favorite Christmas song?"

"Does all of them cover the answer?" I asked then giggled when he playfully nuzzled my neck.

"No. Pick one."

I loved so many songs, but I did have my favorites. "I suppose if I was forced into choosing, I'd go with "Silent Night" or "O Little Town of Bethlehem.""

"Classic and traditional, rather like you."

I hoped his comment meant he liked that I'm not a typical modern woman. I'm fully aware of the fact I can be a little old-fashioned, but it's who I am.

"If I'm counting correctly you have two questions remaining." I snuggled a little closer to him, thrilled by the feeling of resting against him. I couldn't recall a time I'd felt so safe and cherished.

"Then I better make them count," he said. His breath, scented with chocolate, blew across my cheek and I battled a shiver that had nothing to do with the cold. "What are you afraid of, Carol? What forced you back to Christmas Mountain? From what little I know, you left when you were cighteen, no one heard a peep from you for years, then you showed up last November out of the blue. Something had to happen to make you come back all of the sudden."

Something had happened, but he didn't need to know what. The fewer people who knew the reasons for my return, the better. Even if I liked Tim and trusted him, to keep us both safe, some secrets had to remain secret.

"Who says I'm afraid of anything?"

Tim sighed and kissed my cheek. "I don't know if you realize it, but I'm not nearly as stupid as you might think."

When I started to protest, he kissed my cheek again. "It doesn't take a rocket scientist to see you're always on guard. You jump at the slightest noise, you've got martial arts moves that would make a ninja cower in fear, and you never share about yourself, keeping everything intentionally vague. Obviously, you try to disguise the fact you're a beautiful, desirable woman behind your baggy clothes, fake glasses, and a bun that would do a matronly librarian proud."

I started to pull away from him, but he kept one hand on my waist while he reached out and snagged the thick envelope he'd tossed on the blanket earlier.

He opened it, turned it upside down, and half a dozen magazines fell onto my lap, every single one of them with me on the cover.

"Why don't you tell me about your years as a super model, Lyra Levy?"

## *Chapter Ten*

As I stared at the magazines Tim dumped in my lap, flashing red lights erupted in my head like a full-fledged warning of impending doom. How had he figured out who I'd been, what I'd been, the last several years?

He moved so he sat across from me, intently watching my face. Icy fingers closed around me, leaving me half frozen. It had far more to do with the absence of his warmth behind me than the frosty December day.

Since he clearly knew the truth, the time for evasive replies and ambiguous answers had passed.

It wasn't hard to guess where he found the magazines. One was the latest issue of a sports magazine that put out a yearly edition with a model in a swimsuit on the cover. My manager had done a great job keeping my image plastered in magazines and billboards the past year, even though I hadn't posed for a single shot for almost fourteen months.

"You are Lyra Levy, aren't you?" Tim asked. He took his phone from an inside coat pocket and pulled up a photo of me sitting on his lap at the bookstore when he was in the Santa suit. I took the phone from him. It was a cute picture, even if I was irritated at Karen for taking them at the time.

"The first time I met you, I was sure I'd seen you before, but not in a generic face in the Christmas Mountain crowd way. Between your fear of strangers, tendency to hide at the store, and the fact you are gorgeous beyond belief when you aren't dressing like a bag lady, I started wondering if you weren't hiding something. After we took these photos, I went home and compared them to these magazines. No doubt remained that you are Lyra Levy. Want to tell me why you're hiding here?"

I didn't want to tell him, but I didn't really feel like I had a choice at this point.

"You're one of a handful of people who know I'm Lyra. I'd like to keep it that way," I said, giving him a warning look along with his phone.

"I wouldn't share that with anyone, Carol. It's not my story to tell. Not even Nana or Aunt Charli know."

"Thank you," I said with relief. "I suppose if you want the whole story, which is what you've been digging at this afternoon, I might as well give it to you."

He grinned and shifted back around so he was once again sitting with his arms wrapped around me. Call me crazy, but it was easier to spill my guts when a hunky, genuinely kind man held me in his arms.

"Guilty as charged," he said, sounding pleased he'd triumphed in getting the truth out of me. "Why don't you start at the beginning?"

"The beginning is with my parents. My mother was not a beauty by any sense of the word, but she was smart and driven. She never talked about it much, but I got the idea in school she didn't have friends and always felt left out. She blamed it on her looks. I think it had more to do with the fact she was manipulative, shrewd, and ruthless."

"But your dad sounds like he was such a nice guy. How did they connect?" Tim asked, drawing me a little closer.

I took my phone out of my coat pocket, scrolled through photos and brought up one of my family that was taken the Christmas before Dad died. I held it up so Tim could see the screen. My mother was upset Dad insisted on the photo of us standing in front of the Christmas tree. He and I laughed at something he'd said, but Mom wore a trademark scowl.

"I've always thought Mom looked like a female version of David Schwimmer, except not nearly as attractive."

A laugh burst out of Tim, then he gave me a hug. "I'm sorry. I didn't mean to laugh, but I see what you mean."

"Mom had mousy brown hair, small brown

eyes, the figure of a board, and only smiled when she was trying to impress clients or manipulate someone." I pointed to my father. "Dad was born with this horrible birthmark on the right side of his face."

I'd never given a thought to the red discoloration that went from his eyebrow all the way to his chin. He was just my awesome, loving, caring father.

"Most people took one look at him and all they saw was the birthmark. He was very self-conscious about it. I think my mother saw an opportunity because my dad was very handsome, even with the birthmark."

"I see the resemblance between you and him. You think your mother manipulated him into marrying her?"

"Without a single doubt. She'd never admit that's what she did, but I know it. Anyway, when I came along, I think Dad worried I'd have a birthmark and I do, just not where anyone can see it."

"Hmm. A new mystery to unravel," Tim whispered in my ear.

"Don't count on it, buster."

He chuckled and kissed my temple. "Oh, I am, Christmas Carol."

It took effort to ignore the warmth oozing through me at his teasing, but I continued with my story. "Dad always told me my resemblance to his grandmother was uncanny. She was a scandalous flapper back in the day."

Tim leaned around so I could see his face. "I

could totally see you in a flapper outfit. In fact, didn't you have on…" He reached for the magazines I'd set aside.

I smacked at his hands then snuggled back against him. "Either stay focused or I'll stop talking."

"Please continue, Miss Bossy Britches."

I glowered at him over my shoulder. "As I was saying, Dad always said I took after his grandmother who was reportedly beautiful and feisty. His mom was lovely, too. I think my grandmother and mother hated each other. Anyway, by the time I was three, I had a head full of golden-brown curls, blue eyes, and could sing with the best of them, so my mother started entering me in beauty contests. Then the lessons began: dancing lessons, voice lessons, comportment lessons. She cared far less about my education or what I wanted than trying to live vicariously through me since she was always the homely girl in her class. One day, I had enough and ran off after school before she could pick me up to take me to a voice lesson. I ducked into the bookstore when I saw her driving down the street looking for me and Mr. Abernathy offered me a place of refuge. I'm sure half the people in town knew I hid there after school, but I don't think anyone ever said a word to Mom. Twice, my dad came into the store to pick me up when it was snowing, and I knew he was fully aware of my hiding spot."

"I'm glad you had your dad and Mr. Abernathy."

"Me, too." If it hadn't been for them, I'd never

have survived my childhood. "Mom still forced me to compete in beauty pageants and take lessons, but not as frequently. My junior year of high school, she entered me in a teen pageant. I won the state title and went on to compete at the national level. I came in second, but I received offers from five modeling agencies to work for them. I didn't give them much thought although Mom wanted me to pursue them. Then my dad passed away and I needed a means of escape. I just couldn't take life with my mother any longer. I called the agent who reminded me most of my dad. Jason remembered me, offered me a job, and became my manager. The day after I graduated, I left for New York and cut off all contact with Christmas Mountain and my friends here. I needed a fresh start. After I told my mother I was working in a truck stop, I knew she'd blab to everyone in town how I was a failure. When I moved back, I can't tell you how many people asked me when I was going to start working at Prancer's Pancake House. People assume I've done nothing but work as a waitress since I left here."

"Then they're idiots. How can they look at you and not realize you're Lyra?"

Tim's words made me feel better about myself than I had for a while but I shrugged. "People see what they want to see. No one had any idea what I've really done these past years and they would never expect bookish Carol Bennett to be a model. And before you ask, the irony that I ended up in a modeling career due to my mother's interfering influence in my younger years is a sore subject with me."

He grinned. "How did you go from small-town girl to the red-haired Lyra Levy?"

That was a question I sometimes asked myself when I reflected back over my life the past several years.

"Jason said golden hair and blue eyes were too common. His secretary took me to a swanky salon and had them dye my hair red then I got non-prescription green contacts. I don't really have anything wrong with my vision."

"Which I'd like noted that I noticed right away."

"Point for the cowboy," I teased. "After the change in hair color, Jason said I needed a new name to go along with the new look. His wife was the one who came up with Lyra and Jason tacked on Levy. Honestly, I liked having a new look, a new identity, that allowed me to be someone entirely different. I went from posing for a few mediocre campaigns, to being in demand for major designers. And through my work, I was able to travel the world, see fabulous places, and have many wonderful experiences."

"I hear a but in there. What happened?"

As I'd observed when I first met Tim, he was far too perceptive for my own good.

"Two years ago, right before Christmas, a package showed up at my apartment. I'd received gifts from designers I'd worked with as well as friends, so I didn't think anything about a box arriving. When I opened it, there was a note inside with a dozen dead roses that warned me to quit modeling or I'd be sorry. Jason chalked it up to a prank, but it didn't stop there. Whenever I was in New York, strange things would happen at photo shoots. I often had that weird sensation you get when you know you're being watched but can't see anyone spying on you. Jason was convinced I had a stalker and enlisted the police's help in catching him. Then accidents started to happen. A light fell and would have hit me if the makeup artist hadn't shoved me out of the way. A car almost ran over me as I left a photo shoot. Then someone poisoned my coffee and I had to be rushed to the hospital. That's when I decided I'd had enough. Once I recovered my strength enough to work, Jason agreed to my plan to disappear without anyone noticing I'd left. He lined up photo shoots with dozens of companies and designers who'd asked about me posing for one of their ad campaigns, magazines, or promotional pieces. The next six weeks were just a blur. In one day alone, I think I was in three different countries, doing photo shoots in each one."

"Why the brutal schedule?" Tim asked.

I picked up a magazine and glanced at the cover where I was posed on a white sandy beach in Zanzibar. My long red hair was slightly damp, falling in tousled waves around my golden skin while I wore a swimsuit that now made me blush to look at it. I'd changed so much in the last year, into a person I was really beginning to like.

I tossed the magazine back on the stack and looked out at the snow-covered landscape. After all those years of spending my winters in warm climates, I still hadn't adjusted to the cold, but I wouldn't trade being in Christmas Mountain for

145

anything. Not even a beach house on a tropical island.

"Jason wanted there to be a stockpile of images of me so it would appear I was still working. Then I ditched the green contacts, had a salon color my hair brown, packed my things, and disappeared. The one place I could think of to escape to was Christmas Mountain. I drove here all the way from New York and on the way, I called Mr. Abernathy. When he mentioned he wished he could find a buyer for his store so he could retire, it seemed like everything was meant to be. While I'm building a place for myself here, an undercover detective who looks enough like me to be my doppelganger pretends to be me when I'm reportedly back in New York. According to the rumors Jason has kept up the last year, I'm in great demand overseas and rarely back on American soil. Blake, that's the police detective, does a great job of being Lyra."

"Someone is still threatening you?"

"Yes. Jason sends me updates every few months, via coded messages mailed by his youngest daughter at her college campus. The police still haven't caught anyone, but there's been another poisoning attempt, a near hit-and-run, and someone tried to knife Blake back in October when she was walking down the sidewalk in front of my apartment building. She wasn't hurt, but the assailant got away. Threatening letters arrive at the apartment at least once a month with dire warnings. The police have analyzed them and have a few leads, but nothing has panned out so far."

"Oh, Carol, I'm sorry you had to go through all

that, are still dealing with it. No wonder you're so careful and guarded. I can't blame you at all, baby." His lips brushed over my temple.

I wasn't certain if it was the kiss or the way he called me baby that left me so languid I wasn't sure how I'd get on the horse and ride to the house.

"We should probably be getting back," he said, although he made no move to leave. "Any other secrets you need to share?"

Well, I certainly wasn't going to tell him how much I liked him. In truth, I realized I was in love with Tim Burke. During my years of modeling, I'd dated a lot of men. I'd been on the arms of celebrities and even a few royals, but no one made me feel like Tim could with just a look or a touch. And it went far beyond the realm of physical attraction.

Tim made me laugh, challenged my mind, and we had a lot in common, too. He even liked the same books and movies that I enjoyed. Not to mention I loved his grandmother and aunt, but I couldn't tell him any of that. Not until whoever was after me was behind bars.

Granted, I was probably as safe as I could possibly be in Christmas Mountain, but I'd never be able to rest easy until I knew for certain I wouldn't one day wake up and find someone standing over my bed, ready to strangle or suffocate me. The last thing I'd do is put someone I love in jeopardy and that certainly included Tim. Although he looked like he could wrestle a bear and win, I refused to even consider the possibility of things going any further between us until my stalker was no longer a threat.

I turned slightly and picked up the magazines then raised my eyebrows in question. "One of these magazines came out four years ago and these three are from two years past. Where did you find them?" Curiosity kept my gaze pinned on him even when he dropped his eyes from mine. If I wasn't imagining it, I was sure he blushed.

"I, um… well, I kind of…"

"You kind of what?" I asked when he fell silent.

He cleared his throat twice before he spoke. "The first time I saw a photo of Lyra was when I was overseas on a tour of duty. One of the guys had a friend that sent him a box of magazines and he shared with the rest of us. When I saw you on the cover, I don't know what it was. It wasn't just a 'Wow! Look at that beautiful girl' kind of thing. I felt this deep connection to you I can't explain. From then on, if I saw a magazine with your photo on it, I bought it."

"So you've been hankering after Lyra all this time and when you saw me, you what?" I leaned away although he still had his arms around me as I sat glowering at him over my shoulder. "Did you decide you'd found a Lyra look alike and could make do with her?"

The stupidity of being jealous of myself wasn't lost on me, but I couldn't help but wonder if Tim liked me as Carol or because he knew I was Lyra.

Tim picked me up like I weighed next to nothing then set me across his lap. He tipped back his hat and stared at me with such a fierce look in his eyes, I didn't know whether to be afraid or scoot a little closer to him.

"Let me make one thing perfectly clear to you, Carol Bennett. The reason I felt the connection to Lyra had nothing to do with her hair, or her incredible body, or her clothes, it was something I could see in her eyes. Not in the color, but in the depths. Even with all that makeup, she looked kind and there was always a gentleness about her. I bet everyone who met Lyra said she was a nice person."

"Possibly." Truthfully, Jason and some of my friends, like Lacey, used to tease me about being too nice. I still don't think such a thing is possible, though. You can never be too nice, too kind, too caring. Despite my thoughts on the subject, I had been less than kind to Tim when we first met and I regretted every snarky comment I tossed at him.

His hold on me tightened. "The first time I met you, I felt something in here," he said, taking my hand and placing it on his chest. "Even if we didn't exactly get along that first day, I couldn't get you out of my thoughts. Why do you think I went home and dug out all these magazines? I was so fascinated with you I immediately saw the resemblance to Lyra. And for the record, I much prefer blue eyes to green and your sun-kissed hair to red. If I had to choose, I'd pick you, Carol, over a super model any day."

Talk about wooing with words, Tim had just done a stellar job. Before I could utter a reply, his lips captured mine and no more words were needed. That familiar electric jolt rocked through my entire body as the kiss deepened and Tim drew me closer to him. Everything in me shouted that this was where I'd always belonged, where I should always stay. Too involved in the kiss to tell the voice in my head to hush, I returned Tim's fervor until I was sure the sparks between us would set the trees on fire.

Finally, he pulled back just enough to rest his forehead against mine. "Any doubt about who holds my heart and my love?" The husky rumble of his voice made my insides quiver.

"No. No doubts," I whispered then pulled his head down to mine. Eager for more of his kisses they provided a mind-numbing distraction as I avoided telling him I loved him, too.

The ringing of his cell phone interrupted our impassioned connection. He was grumbling something I couldn't hear as he yanked the phone from his pocket.

"What's wrong, Nana?"

I couldn't help but grin when I realized his ringtone had been "Grandma Got Run Over By A Reindeer." I wondered if Nancy knew he'd set that as the way to identify her calls. If she did, she most likely thought it was hilarious.

"No. We'll be back soon."

He rolled his eyes as he looked at me and I pressed my lips together to keep from giggling.

"Yes, Nana. Okay. See you in a bit." He tucked the phone back inside his coat pocket, kissed me on the nose, then set me on the blanket. He stood and grinned down at me. "Nana has threatened to send out a search party if I don't bring you back to the house soon. She's convinced I'll let you get frostbite if we stay out much longer."

The heat sizzling between the two of us could have kept me warm in the middle of a blizzard, but I definitely wouldn't explain that detail to Nancy.

Tim held out a hand and pulled me to my feet when I took it. He stuffed the magazines back in the envelope and returned it along with the thermos to his saddle bags while I folded the blanket. He rolled it up and tied it behind his saddle, then led me around to mount Jude.

"Need any help?" he asked as he handed me the reins.

"I think I've got it." I swung into the saddle with ease even though my backside and thighs protested.

"Oh, you've got it, all right," he said, winking at me before he walked over to Rowan and mounted.

Uncertain as to what, exactly, he thought I had, I let it drop as we rode back to the house. It took a while before I thawed out, but the Christmas tea (a blend of black tea with vanilla and nutmeg that tasted a lot like eggnog) and spice bundt cake topped with a buttery sauce Charli served helped.

When we finished the snack, Nancy insisted I stay and help them finish decorating the towering fir tree that had to be at least fifteen feet tall. Tim stood on a ladder above me while I handed him ornaments and Nancy told stories about each one. I studied an ornament clearly made by a child.

"Tim made that in first grade," Nancy said, pointing to the clothespin reindeer I held.

"It's adorable." I handed it to Tim with a warm

smile. For a minute, I thought he might slide right down the ladder and give me a kiss. Instead, he took the ornament with a smoldering look that made me rethink my plan to tell him to stay away from me for a while.

As we finished decorating the tree, Tim asked me to sing a few carols. I discovered he had a rich baritone that complimented my alto voice. I also learned Nancy can't carry a tune worth beans but Charli did a good job singing soprano.

Nancy and Charli insisted I stay for dinner (which was fabulous). After I helped Charli with the dishes, I knew it was time to leave. Charli boxed up a piece of the chocolate cream pie we had for dessert and sent it with me to enjoy later.

"If you keep feeding me like this, I'm going to be as round as Mrs. Claus," I said, giving Charli a hug and then Nancy.

"I don't think you have a thing to worry about, darling," Nancy said with a smile. "We're just glad you came out today."

"Me, too. I had a wonderful time and appreciate the delicious meal. You ladies have a peaceful evening and a great week. If you come into town, stop by the store."

"We will, Carol," Nancy said with a wave as Tim walked with me out of the kitchen and down the hall to the front door.

He held my coat as I slipped it on then yanked on his coat and opened the door. The air was bitingly cold, but Tim dropped his arm around my shoulders as we walked over to my car, keeping me warm.

I started the engine but slid back out while the heater kicked on. Tim opened his arms and I went straight into them, hugging him tightly. Goodness only knew if I'd ever have the opportunity again.

The words I needed to say were lodged in my throat like a glob of school paste (not that I ever ate it as a kid), but I'd already waited far too long to push Tim away.

I wracked my brain for the best thing to say. Tim brushed a thumb over my cheek then kissed me so tenderly and sweetly, my whole body felt like a lump of putty. Never in my life had I experienced such a kiss or such a longing to love and be loved by another human being.

"Tim," I whispered, eyes still closed, lingering in his embrace.

"I meant what I said earlier. You're beautiful, intelligent, fun, witty, successful, and amazing. I know it seems too soon, but I've never felt like this about anyone. Carol, I really do love you."

*I love you* was on the tip of my tongue but I bit it before the words spilled out of my mouth. I did love Tim. More than I would have imagined possible since we'd only known each other a few short weeks, but he was everything I could ever want in a man, even if I was just now realizing it. It was because of how much I loved him that I had to let him go.

"Tim, I…" I still couldn't bring myself to say something that would hurt him. I stopped, attempting to collect my thoughts. The speech I'd prepared in my head seemed trite as I recalled what I planned to say. Tim deserved better than that, more than that. And no matter how much easier it would have made things, I refused to lie to him.

His expression changed from happy to disappointed, obviously assuming I didn't feel the same. "It's okay, Carol. You don't have to say anything. I shouldn't have said anything. I promise I won't turn into a weird stalker, or anything."

"I know you won't, Tim. I just need some time." That much was true. My head felt like it was spinning in circles. Between the holidays, my store, dredging up family memories, and falling in love with Tim, I was about to drown in emotions. A little time away from him would help give me perspective and clear my head. Then there was that whole keep him safe thing, too.

"I can give you all the time you need, Carol. Just don't forget about me."

"How could I forget about you? Tim Burke makes a strong impression that sticks with you."

A hollow laugh burst out of him, one that held no mirth. "That's what I'm afraid is the problem."

"No, Tim. It's me. I just need…"

"Time," he said, looking so dejected, I almost admitted how much I cared for him, loved him.

Instead, I kissed his cheek, climbed inside my toasty vehicle, and headed home. I didn't allow myself the luxury of tears until I sank up to my chin in a bathtub full of hot water and my favorite bath salts.

Then I couldn't seem to stop crying.

## *Chapter Eleven*

"What happened to your hunkalicious cowboy?" Karen asked after the customer she was assisting left with a bag full of brightly-wrapped packages. "I haven't seen him around the store lately."

"We're taking a break," I said, which was true. The reasons behind it and how miserable it made me were something I wouldn't discuss, though.

Karen just raised her left eyebrow and shook her head. "Girl, guys like him don't come along every day, or even every decade. It takes a special kind of man to wear a Santa suit and let dozens of children swarm him when he had no prior knowledge that's how he'd spend his Saturday morning."

"I know," I said on a sigh. Tim was special. Wonderful. In fact, I'd been mentally composing a list of words to describe him when Karen interrupted me. So far, I'd come up with terrific, tantalizing, talented, tasty, tender, tremendous, tolerant, troublesome, and tough. I should get out my thesaurus and see how many more I could add.

Or, I could focus on the fact Christmas was a few days away and my store was packed with shoppers.

I smiled at Karen and patted her arm as I walked past her on my way to stock shelves. "It'll be fine, Karen."

As I watched a mother with two precious little girls, I felt a sudden yearning to have children of my own. The face that popped into my head when I thought about children was Tim's. He'd proven beyond a shadow of a doubt he'd be a fabulous dad not to mention an amazing husband.

But I was not in the market for happily ever afters. At least not at the moment.

After I left Aspen Grove Ranch the day I told Tim I needed time, I assumed things were over between us.

Instead, he'd been incredibly sweet. He'd mailed me a hilarious Christmas card and had signed it, "Yours, Tim."

One morning I let Hemi outside and found a box with my name on it leaning against the door. Inside was a note from Tim telling me to enjoy Charli's breakfast. I was excited to discover a thermos of her minty hot chocolate and a foil-wrapped package of chocolate chip muffins that were surprisingly still warm.

Yesterday afternoon, I'd looked up from the cash register to see the florist carrying in a beautiful arrangement of Christmas greens and red and white flowers. With it was a basket filled with an assortment of holiday teas, rich chocolates, delicious cookies, and a note from Tim that simply said he was thinking of me.

Marilyn had been there at the time and nearly pestered the patience right out of me asking question after question.

I took the basket and arrangement up to my apartment and sent Tim a text, thanking him for his thoughtfulness. This morning, I savored every drop of one of the teas he'd sent that was a luscious blend of vanilla and cinnamon with nutty undertones. And I may have eaten a package of chocolate-dipped butter cookies for breakfast.

Admittedly, I missed Tim, missed his silly text messages and the calls we'd gotten into the habit of making each evening at the end of our day. I missed the warmth of his presence and the joy of his smile. And then there was the way he looked at me, eyes smoldering, like I was the most magnificent woman he'd ever met.

I definitely had it bad for Tim. Here I was with Christmas fast approaching, a booming business, friends all around me, and I was miserable. All I could think about was Tim and how much I longed to be with him.

Ugh! I needed to get out of my own head and concentrate on helping the customers waiting in line. By the time the store closed that evening, I was an exhausted mess.

Not even indulging in another cup of tea along with a hot, scented bath helped, although I did fall asleep in the tub. I might have spent the whole night there if Hemi hadn't taken it upon himself to tell me it was time for bed. He meowed so loudly it startled me awake. I banged my ankle on the faucet as I jumped up, then had to execute a few fancy moves to keep from falling on the slick floor when I splashed water all over.

The angry glares I tossed at the cat didn't bother him in the least. He merely sat on the bath rug licking his paw, as though he hadn't disturbed me at all.

I remained tense, quiet, and inwardly peevish the next few days.

Christmas Eve morning I awoke after another restless night with the strangest feeling something was off, like something had happened. I grabbed my cell phone off the nightstand and checked, but I had no messages. I did a double-take when I actually noticed the time. It was only four-thirty.

I flopped back against the pillows, but after five minutes, it was clear I wasn't going to get more rest.

Tossing back the covers, I got up and started to dress in my workout clothes, but changed my mind. I took a long shower, allowed myself the luxury of curling my hair, and applied a little makeup. I tugged on a pair of my favorite jeans (a gift from a happy designer), pulled on a cream sweater (one I'd picked up in Scotland), and spritzed on expensive perfume. After I slid my feet into a pair of flats, I wandered into my kitchen.

I made a cup of tea (cinnamon and clove-infused green tea), then sat on the couch and flipped on the television. I turned to a holiday movie and tried to get lost in the story, but my thoughts tumbled around and over each other. The feeling something was wrong just kept getting stronger and stronger.

I turned off the television, picked up my cup of tea, and almost tripped over Hemi as he wound between my feet, purring.

"Come on, furball," I said in a teasing tone. "Let's go see if anything is amiss in the store."

Together, Hemi and I made our way downstairs. I'd left the Christmas lights on and they glowed cheerfully through the early morning darkness. Rather than turn on the overhead lights, I made my way down the hallway, let Hemi outside and fed him, then returned to the front of the store.

I turned on all the lights and looked up and down every aisle, searched every cranny, and discovered Mia asleep in an overstuffed chair in the biography section. How had that little imp managed to hide while I locked up last night?

She looked so peaceful, curled onto her side with her purple hair fanned across her cheek.

Uncertain what to do, I went upstairs to make a real breakfast and even unearthed a frozen can of orange juice concentrate that I mixed. When the food was ready, I set the table then went to get Mia.

She was still sleeping soundly when I returned. I hated to wake her, but I couldn't help but think her family would wonder what happened to her. She still hadn't told me much about what was going on at home or why she sought out the refuge of the store. In time, I was sure she'd confide in me, but I intended to get a few answers while we ate breakfast.

"Mia," I said softly, placing a hand on her shoulder. "Mia." I gave her a gentle shake.

Her eyes popped open and she lunged to her feet, looking like she'd just been caught robbing the bank.

"It's okay, Mia. I made breakfast. Why don't you come upstairs and eat? Maybe you can tell me what made you decide to spend the night in my store."

Mutely, she nodded and followed me upstairs.

"Cool," she said as she walked around the end of the bookcase and saw my apartment door.

"This is confidential. I prefer people not know how to find my apartment."

Another nod as we walked inside my living room. I left the door open in case Hemi wanted to return upstairs and turned to find Mia glancing around with a look of awe on her face. I had garlands and ribbons hanging all over, as well as numerous Christmas decorations. My white couch had a red and white throw tossed over one end and red pillows accenting it. The tree (which had taken Herculean effort to get up the stairs and into the apartment), decorated with ornaments I'd collected from around the world, filled the space with a wonderful fir scent while the aromas of bacon and cinnamon (from the pot of tea I made), wafted in the air.

"It's amazing, Miss Bennett," Mia said, turning

to me with a bright smile.

"Thank you." I pointed to my bathroom. "If you want to wash up, I've got everything ready."

She hurried into the bathroom and closed the door. I went into the kitchen and dished up the food, setting it on the table. Mia walked into the kitchen as I poured the steaming, fragrant tea into two teacups. The dishes had belonged to my dad's mother and were one thing I'd taken with me when I left home. They'd stayed safely packed away in a box all the years I was modeling, but when I moved into the apartment above the bookstore, I took them out and used them whenever I had a friend visiting (which wasn't often), or I wanted my meal to feel a little special (again, not often).

The creamy dishes with deep red roses looked particularly festive on the forest green tablecloth I'd spread on the table.

Wide-eyed, Mia took a seat. Her gaze flicked from the beautiful arrangement Tim had sent to the dishes, to the plates filled with food. On a good day I feel I've accomplished wonders if I make soup without scorching it in the pan, but I can cook bacon in the oven, and make French toast. I happened to have a bowl of fresh berries and a can of spray whipping cream along with a bottle of maple syrup to round out the simple meal.

"This looks great, Miss Bennett. Thank you," Mia said.

"You're welcome, Mia. Would you like sugar for your tea?"

At her nod, I passed her the sugar bowl and watched as she stirred a heaping spoon into the amber liquid. She drained her glass of juice then ate two pieces of French toast smothered in whipping cream and berries along with four pieces of bacon while I mostly toyed with my teacup. I still had a feeling something awful was going to happen and I didn't think it had anything to do with Mia.

"It's very good," she said, taking a sip of the still steaming tea. "Yum. That tastes like Christmas."

"It's a Christmas blend," I said, smiling at her. I fought down the urge to brush a stray lock of hair behind her ear. Maternal urges I didn't even know I possessed had burst to life recently and I had an idea no amount of coaxing or ignoring them would get them to quietly retreat to the little corner of my being where they'd been hiding all these years.

Mia eyed the food, so I nudged the bacon and French toast toward her. "Help yourself."

She took two more pieces of bacon and another piece of the golden-brown bread. "Thanks for not calling the cops," she said as she drizzled syrup over the French toast.

"Why would I call the police?" I asked, taking a bite of my toast. It was pretty good, if I do say so myself.

"Because I'm in your store and not supposed to be here. I didn't steal anything though," she said, tossing me a panicked look. "I promise."

"I believe you, Mia. However, it would be good to know why you spent the night here."

She hurriedly stuffed a big bite of toast into her mouth, effectively postponing the need to answer.

I ate my toast and bacon while she finished her

food and tea.

"Is everything okay?" I asked, growing more concerned over the worry gnawing at my stomach like a dog chewing on a juicy bone.

She shook her head as she wiped her mouth on a paper napkin imprinted with holly berries. Tears welled in her eyes and spilled down her cheeks.

"Mia? What in the world is wrong?" I placed a comforting hand on her arm.

The tears were coming so hard and fast, I knew she couldn't speak. I helped her to her feet, led her to the couch, took a seat beside her, and wrapped my arms around her as sobs wracked through her. She seemed so young and fragile as I held her. When the storm lessoned, I grabbed a box of tissues I kept on the table at the end of the couch and handed it to her.

She blew her nose, mopped at her wet cheeks, and released a heavy sigh. "I'm sorry, Miss Bennett."

"Call me Carol."

"I'm sorry, Carol, but I just couldn't go home last night. I just couldn't."

"Is someone at home hurting you? Abusing you?" Fearful of what she might reveal, I felt a responsibility to unearth the truth for her sake. If I could do something to help her, I would.

"Not like that, not what you're thinking," she said then sighed again. "It's my dad. He drinks. A lot."

Ah. Now we were getting somewhere. "Does he threaten you? Yell at you?"

"No. Dad wouldn't do that. He drinks to

forget."

"Forget what?" I asked, trying to piece the puzzle together.

"My mom. She died in a car wreck when I was two and my brother was nine. Dad couldn't deal with a toddler, so I went to live with my grandma in Missoula. She passed away right before Halloween." She dabbed at more tears.

"I'm sorry, Mia. It must have been so hard to lose your grandmother."

She nodded and took a deep breath. "Grandma was the one who raised me, but when she died, I had to come live with Dad and Marcus. My brother is awesome, but Dad is just… sad."

"Oh, Mia. I know how hard it is to lose people you love." I gave her another tight hug. "Does your dad own McBride's garage?"

"Yeah. Marcus has been managing it since he was sixteen. It just seems like it's more than Dad can handle when he spends so much time drinking." Mia grabbed more tissues and wiped her face. "Dad isn't mean to me or anything like that, but it's been hard moving in with him and Marcus. When I lived with Grandma, she always had a snack ready for me after school and we'd talk about my day then make dinner together. She helped me with my homework and listened, really listened, to my problems. Mostly, my dad ignores me. He comes home drunk and quiet almost every night. Marcus is the one who pays the bills, gives me lunch money, watches out for me, and buys the groceries. He's trying to run the garage and take online classes in business management in the evenings, so he's always busy."

"He sounds like a good brother," I said, waiting for Mia to get to the reason why she spent the night in my store.

"He's the best. Grandma taught me how to cook a little and do laundry and stuff. I try to help around the house so Marcus doesn't have to do everything."

"That's good of you."

She started twisting the tissues in her hands into a skinny rope. "Grandma always made Christmas really special, but Marcus doesn't have time and Dad just doesn't care. We don't have a tree or stockings or even a wreath. I made Dad and Marcus gifts, but I don't think either of them will remember it's Christmas. Yesterday was the last day of school until after New Year's. I just couldn't go home to our house last night. It's so depressing."

This poor child was breaking my heart. Grateful no one was hurting her, at least physically, I knew being ignored was its own form of abuse. Not only that, but trying to adjust to the loss of a beloved grandmother who had, from the sounds of it, fulfilled the roles of both mother and father, then having to move to a new place where she didn't feel loved had to be so challenging and painful. At least she had a caring brother. He was probably struggling to keep his head above water, too.

Thoughts of all the things I could possibly do to help raced through my head. I'm sure I could enlist some of my friends to give Mia a merry Christmas.

But first, she needed to go home. If her father wasn't concerned about her, I'm sure her brother had to be frantic.

"Does your brother or dad know where you are?"

"No," Mia said in a small voice. "I forgot my cell phone in my locker at school."

I handed her more tissues then stood. "Come on. Let's get you home. Won't your brother be worried?"

"Probably." She didn't make eye contact with me as she stood.

"Why don't you wash your face while I set the dishes in the sink, then I'll take you home."

"Okay."

I hurried to the kitchen and cleaned up from breakfast with record speed. I wouldn't have bothered, but I had visions of returning to find Hemi on the table, lapping up bacon grease. That alone was enough to make me fill the sink with hot soapy water and leave the dishes to soak.

Mia came into the kitchen and offered to help, so we washed and dried the dishes and put them away.

I knew she was stalling and I let her. I glanced at the clock which showed it was half past six. Time for her to face the music.

"Ready to go?" I asked, giving her shoulders a hug as we walked out of the kitchen into the living room. I kicked off my flats and jerked on a pair of snow boots, then grabbed my coat and purse.

She picked up the backpack she'd set by the door and slung it over her shoulder then marched down the stairs with all the enthusiasm of one about to face a firing squad.

"If you want to wait in here, I'll go warm up

my car," I said, pulling the keys from my purse.

"I only live a few blocks from here. I can walk," she said, standing to the side as I unlocked the door and opened it.

She shuffled out onto the snow-dusted sidewalk.

"I'll walk with you," I said, quickly locking the door and waiting for her to lead the way. As we strolled through the early morning darkness, illuminated by Christmas lights and the street lamps, I talked about The Christmas Extravaganza planned at the community center tomorrow that I'd be singing in and invited her to come.

We turned down a residential street and she walked to the gate of a house that at one time had probably been quite nice. The paint, or what was left of it, was peeling off the siding, and the porch steps sagged, like they needed repaired or replaced. At least the snow hid any other defects.

All the lights were on in the house, so I didn't question if anyone was awake. Resigned, Mia sighed and her shoulders drooped as she opened the gate. The rusty hinges squealed in protest, but she forged ahead with me right behind her, my hand on her shoulder for reassurance.

We hadn't even made it to the steps when the door flew open and a man I vaguely recognized from my childhood years as the best mechanic in town raced down the steps. Tears streamed down his sunken cheeks as he grabbed Mia and hugged her close to him.

"Oh, baby girl. I've been worried to death. Oh, Mia." He held her tight, as though he'd never let her go.

A young man who bore a strong resemblance to Mr. McBride ran down the steps and wrapped his arms around both of them.

"Mia June McBride, if you ever disappear like that again, I'll, I'll…" Marcus's voice cracked with emotion and he blinked his eyes several times, clearly trying to hold back the tears. "I'm so glad you came home."

All three of them were crying and it seemed like such a personal, intimate family moment, but I felt compelled to stay to offer an explanation of why I was with Mia. Finally, the three McBrides turned to look at me.

"You're the bookstore lady," Marcus said. He swiped his sleeve across his face to do away with the tears then wiped his hand on the seat of his jeans before he held it out to me.

"You must be Marcus," I said with a smile as I shook his hand. "I'm Carol Bennett and I own Rudolph's Reads. I've gotten to know Mia a little bit recently."

Mia glanced at me then at her father. "I hid in the store and spent the night but Carol didn't know I was there. She found me this morning and made breakfast for me then brought me home. I left my phone at school by accident and I'm sorry." By the time Mia finished, she was crying again.

"Mia is always welcome at the store and if there is anything I can do to help, I hope you'll let me know. For now, I think you all could use some time to talk things through. Merry Christmas." Slowly, I backed away from the group.

I was almost to the squeaky gate when Mr. McBride hurried over and clasped my hand between both of his. He was almost as tall as me, built like a wrestler, and in surprisingly good shape, all things considered. He reeked of beer, but his bloodshot eyes appeared clear, not dazed by alcohol. I could see gratitude in his smile and regret in his eyes.

Maybe Mia's stunt would be the wake-up call he needed to let go of his grief and move on with life. "Thank you for bringing my little girl home. I'd die if anything happened to her."

Emotion was about to overtake me, so I smiled and nodded my head. "I'm glad I could help. She really is welcome at the store anytime. I enjoy having her there."

"If you ever need your car worked on, you bring it in, no charge. Ever." Mr. McBride backed up a step. "I can't repay you for seeing after Mia."

"I had no idea she was at the store until I turned on the lights this morning." I lowered my voice so Mia couldn't hear. "She's grieving her grandmother, struggling to find her way at a new school, and just needs to know she is loved and supported at home."

Mr. McBride nodded, his eyes welling with tears. "Things will be better now. I promise."

I grinned. "I'll hold you to that. I fully expect Mia to give me a report after the holidays."

The girl ran over to me and gave me a hug. "Thank you, Carol."

"You're welcome, honey. Have a very Merry Christmas." I kissed her cheek, intent on making sure Christmas arrived at the McBride home.

I turned and walked out of the yard, but stopped to watch as Mr. McBride hugged both of his children to him.

As I stood on that snowy sidewalk, watching them, watching the three of them find hope and love, my qualms about being with Tim suddenly melted away.

What I felt for him wasn't something that came along every day. It was a once-in-a-lifetime love that I'd stupidly been willing to sacrifice because of something that may or may not ever happen. The odds of the lunatic in New York ever finding me in Montana were practically non-existent. Was I really willing to spend the rest of my life alone if that's how long it took for the police to catch him?

I'd spent the last year alone, hiding from myself and the world. Before that, I hid behind the persona of Lyra Levy, letting very few people see the real me.

It was time to let go of my fears, embrace who I was, and move on.

With Tim, if he'd still have me. I took out my phone and sent him a text.

*I'm begging for forgiveness. I've had all the time I need to realize what I really want and need is you. Can we talk?*

He was most likely out feeding and doing chores, so I knew it would be a while before he replied to my text.

In the meantime, I had Christmas to deliver to one purple-haired girl.

## *Chapter Twelve*

Determined to do all I could to give the McBride family a lovely Christmas, I started planning out the details in my head as I walked away from their home.

Filled with excitement at the prospect of playing Santa to Mia, I still felt an overwhelming sense of dread. I couldn't explain it, couldn't define it, and worry settled over me like a wet blanket on a freezing day. I didn't feel like the anxiety had anything to do with Tim, although I was incredibly anxious as I waited for his response to my text.

This was something different, something so vague yet undeniably disturbing I couldn't shake the horrible feeling.

Rather than dwell on it, I marched into

Prancer's Pancake House where I found the owner of the tree lot and cajoled him into delivering a tree to the McBride family as soon as he finished eating breakfast.

I saw one of Christmas Mountain's police officers walk in and rushed over to let her know Mia was safe at home in case they'd been looking for her. Apparently, they'd been searching for her since Marcus called them when Mia never came home for dinner.

Everyone who could hear the conversation seemed relieved, so I decided to be bold as I moved to a spot by the door where everyone could see me and whistled. All eyes turned my way.

"For those of you who don't know, Mia McBride is thirteen, recently lost her grandmother, and moved here to Christmas Mountain. She's afraid Christmas is going to pass her by this year. What do you say we show the McBride family what this community is all about?" My heart swelled amid the cheers and promises to help in my campaign to bring Christmas to the McBride's door.

After speaking to a few business owners, I left the restaurant and hurried to the grocery store. There, I ordered a turkey dinner in a box, the ones that come with a basic dinner for four, then at the bakery, I chose an assortment of pastries for the family to enjoy for breakfast along with a pumpkin pie and a chocolate layer cake. I paid one of the boys who bagged groceries twenty bucks to run the meal over to the family when he got off work. He was friends with Aiden, so I trusted him to get the job done.

On my way back to the bookstore, I sent text messages to my friends, telling them what I was doing. Inside the warmth of Rudolph's Reads, I tossed my coat and purse on the front counter, picked up a large empty box I hadn't yet hauled to the recycle bin, and started filling it with gifts for the McBride family. Of course, I added books for each of them, but I included a few puzzles they could work on as a family as well as two of my favorite board games. I added a snow globe and a few other decorations, tucked in one of my special boxes of Christmas tea and a box of my prized chocolates, then added three holiday mugs.

At my frenzied running around the store, Hemi wandered out and jumped onto the counter where he could watch as I continued adding more goodies to the box. When it was filled to the brim, I taped the box shut and wrapped it, finishing it with a festive bow and a Rudolph's Reads label. Hastily, I wrote a note to Mia in a Christmas card, taping it to the top of the box.

By then, people started showing up with things they wanted to give the McBride family. I'd told everyone my store could be a drop-off point, but only until noon. I wanted to deliver the goodies then. If Tim was agreeable to my plans, I intended to close the store early and spend the rest of the day out at the ranch with him, Nancy, and Charli.

People who'd never set foot in my store arrived with tins of toffee, Christmas decorations, and more. Lonnie Peterson, a prolific knitter, even rolled her wheelchair in to deliver three scarves.

When Miles Wilson popped in and gruffly

handed me a wooden Merry Christmas sign, I almost cried. This was what community and home and Christmas was all about. In spite of his blustering, I kissed his cheek and handed him a cup of hot apple cider before he escaped back out into the cold.

Marilyn, who was working that morning, made a call and soon a group of senior citizens arrived carrying three hand-made stockings stuffed with goodies.

"Thank you," I said, hugging each one of them, then Marilyn.

The store was packed, the noise level somewhere between a rock concert and jet engines, when I felt my phone vibrate in the pocket of my jeans.

Desperately hoping it was Tim, my stomach dropped to my feet when I saw a number I recognized but hadn't heard from in more than a year.

Trying not to panic, I raced upstairs, taking the steps two at a time and running into my apartment. In my haste to take Mia home, I'd forgotten to shut the door and pull the panel across the end of the bookcase. Goodness only knew how many people had wandered in and out of my private space this morning.

Slightly out of breath, I answered the phone on the fourth ring. "Jason! Merry Christmas!"

"It is a Merry Christmas," he said. His voice sounded jolly rather than ready to report something dire. "We got him, Carol. We got him!"

"What happened?" I asked, knowing exactly to

whom he referred. The stalker. My stalker.

"He ramped up his efforts to do you in during the last week. Blake was so ready to be done with all this, and I'm sure you are, too. I purposely leaked details that you were back in New York for the holidays and then made sure the paparazzi had many opportunities to take photos of Blake coming and going from stores, restaurants, even a holiday concert. Of course, no one got close enough to see it wasn't really Lyra. Blake does a good job of wearing big sunglasses and hats and keeping her profile to the camera which is where you really look so much alike."

Aware of Jason's tendency to ramble when he was excited or nervous, I interrupted. "How did she catch him?"

"Each time she went out, something would happen. He even shot an arrow at her which hit one of the annoying paparazzi in the butt. Couldn't have happened to a nicer guy."

I grinned, waiting for Jason to continue.

"Anyway, she stayed in the apartment this past week. We were hoping he'd get really brazen and try breaking in, which he did. Blake made it easy for him and left the door unlocked. Two officers stayed in the apartment, too, for her safety. They waited until he picked up a pillow and placed it over Blake's face before they cuffed him and took him in." Jason paused. "You won't believe who it is."

"Who?"

"Curtis Devoe."

I sank onto the couch, almost sliding off the cushion before I caught myself and flopped back against the seat. Curtis Devoe had been a college student interning for a famous photographer when I first started working with big-name clients. He'd seemed sweet and harmless, although he never knew Lyra Levy wasn't my real name. Jason told me to guard that secret like my life depended on it. And it had.

I'd dated Curtis a few times, but he'd gotten rather clingy, then his internship ended and I assumed that was the end of it. Evidently, I'd been completely wrong.

"But why, Jason? I don't understand?"

"I didn't either until Blake discovered he had a juvenile record of stalking a girl in high school to the point her parents moved away in the middle of the night with no forwarding address to get rid of him. Want to guess what she looked like?"

"Red hair and green eyes," I whispered.

"Bingo. Anyway, I called as soon as Blake assured me he'd be spending a long, long time in jail for attempted murder among many other charges."

Stunned and overwhelmed by the realization the ordeal with my stalker was finally over, I struggled not to burst into tears.

"Oh, and Blake said to thank you. She said it was the best undercover case she'd ever worked."

"She's more than welcome. I appreciate all she did to catch Curtis." I'd told Jason to give Blake anything she wanted from my expansive closet and I happily footed the bill for tickets for her to attend concerts, dine in exclusive restaurants, and enjoy things like pedicures at ritzy salons. Anything that perpetuated the myth that Lyra was out and about in New York, having a wonderful time.

I still couldn't wrap my head around the notion that a boy I'd once thought was nice, albeit slightly weird, wanted to kill me.

"Are you okay?" Jason finally asked when I remained silent.

"I am… I will be." Relief flooded through me. I no longer had to fear someone showing up one day, intent on doing harm. I could live wherever I wanted, however I wanted.

"So, will you come back to New York soon?" Jason asked.

The lure of the lifestyle I'd once enjoyed was there, but not with the strength I'd anticipated. A far different life, one with the man I loved, beckoned to me. In a heartbeat, I'd give up jet-setting around the world, being a person of influence, and making more money than I could spend in a lifetime just to hear Tim say he loved me. Even if he wanted nothing to do with me, I no longer held any interest in being Lyra Levy.

Like I'd told Tim, Christmas Mountain was my home and the place where I most wanted to stay.

"No, Jason. I won't be coming back soon. I don't know how to tell you this, but I…"

"You don't want to be Lyra Levy anymore," he said.

I could picture his fatherly scowl, one I'd seen many times over the years of working with him. Jason had been like a beloved uncle to me from the day I arrived in New York. I'd eaten many meals at his home, attended his children's school plays and graduations. I'd miss him, miss his whole family, but I no longer belonged in New York City. Not when my heart would always be in Montana.

"No, I don't. I'm sorry, Jason. I'm sure this causes…"

He cut me off. "Don't give it a thought, Carol. I knew this day would come eventually. You might have moved to the big city, but you'll always be a small-town girl at heart. Let me guess, you've met someone."

I grinned. "I have, although I'm not so sure he still wants me after I kind of pushed him away."

"It's Christmas! Believe in miracles and who knows what might happen."

"Thanks, Jason, for everything. Will you give Addie and the girls a hug from me?"

"Of course. Why don't I check back in after the holidays? We can talk about how to quietly retire Lyra and then there's your apartment to sell and all those details."

"After Christmas would be great. Thank you, again, Jason. You've been wonderful and in case I never said it, I appreciate you so much."

"I know you do, kid. Now go find that cowboy and have a merry Christmas."

A laugh rolled out of me. "I never said he was a cowboy."

Jason chuckled. "Isn't everyone there? Bye, kiddo."

I stared at my phone for a long moment, processing everything that had happened since I ran up the stairs.

The feeling of dread that had settled over me

that morning magically dissipated. I was free!

With an excited squeal, I did a happy dance around my apartment then hurried back downstairs. My only thought was to tell Tim, but the store full of people brought me up short.

I glanced at the clock. I still had an hour and a half before I could leave.

Marilyn was swamped at the cash register, so I hurried over, trying to push Tim from my thoughts. It was impossible, though.

When I still hadn't heard from Tim as the clock drew close to noon, I decided to drive out to the ranch. If he wanted to tell me he never wanted to see me again, I needed to hear it in person. But first, I had a car load of happiness to deliver to Mia.

Aiden and Josie had both come in to work for a few hours, so the two of them helped me load my car while Marilyn waited on the last customers in the store. At noon on the dot, I wished them all a happy holiday, made sure Hemi was set with plenty of food and water, then locked the door to the store.

All three members of the McBride family rushed out to greet me when I walked up the steps carrying the big box of goodies from my store. Mr. McBride took it from me while Mia hugged me and talked excitedly about a tree showing up at their door. Marcus had climbed up in the attic and brought down boxes of decorations that hadn't seen the light of day for ten years.

"There are a few more things in my car, if you don't mind helping carry them inside," I said to Marcus. He and Mia followed me to the back of my SUV and both of them gaped at all the boxes filled with gifts, treats, and surprises.

"Thank you!" Mia said, hugging me again.

"The community decided you needed a real Christmas Mountain holiday," I said to Mia, my arm around her shoulders. "Enjoy every bit of it."

"I don't know what to say," Mr. McBride said as he stepped beside me. Since I'd been there earlier that morning, he'd showered and the beard he'd worn was gone. His eyes were bright as he grabbed a big box and stared from it to me. "We can pay for all this."

"No, Mr. McBride. This is the community saying Merry Christmas. Maybe someday you can pass it on to someone else who needs a little holiday cheer."

He nodded and turned away, but not before I saw the tears welling in his eyes.

It didn't take long to unload my SUV and be on my way to the ranch. In spite of the cold, my palms felt sweaty as I stepped out of my vehicle and started down the front walk. Brutus loped around the corner of the house and woofed in greeting when he recognized me. After giving him several good scratches and getting my chin licked as a thank you, I jogged up the steps and rang the doorbell.

It only took a moment for the door to open and Nancy to welcome me with a surprised smile.

"Darling! I wasn't sure we'd see you anytime soon. Charli and I hoped you'd still accept our invitation to join us for dinner tonight or tomorrow."

"I would love to accept, but first I need to

speak with Tim. Is he around?"

Nancy sighed and motioned me inside the house. "That poor boy. Today has been one disaster after another. Something spooked the cattle in the east pasture and they knocked down the fence. Tim, Jack, and the boys spent hours rounding up the cattle since some of them had wandered halfway up the mountain into the trees then they had to fix the fence. Tim barely returned from that when a neighbor called and needed help getting his vehicle out of the ditch. The dear old gent is in his eighties and slid off the road when he tried to turn down his driveway. Thank goodness Mr. Anderson had his cell phone with him. On his way back from that, Tim found a half-starved horse wandering down the road with multiple cuts. It isn't one we recognize and has no markings to identify it, but it's in bad shape. Tim's been down at the barn with it waiting for the vet to arrive."

"Oh," was all I could think to say. Tim wasn't intentionally avoiding me which made me feel marginally better.

"Come to the kitchen and have a cup of tea. I'm sure he'll be in soon," Nancy said, leading the way down the hall.

"It's so nice to see you, Carol. Happy Christmas Eve," Charli said, glancing over her shoulder at me as she stood at the stove stirring something in a saucepan. The aroma of spices hung in the air and my stomach growled. I hadn't taken time to eat lunch and the one piece of French toast and bacon I'd nibbled at for breakfast had worn off hours ago.

"This girl is hungry, Charli." Nancy tattled.

"I'm fine." Embarrassment stained my cheeks bright red when my stomach growled a second time.

Nancy laughed and motioned for me to take a seat at the table.

Hesitantly, I removed my coat and scarf then washed my hands at the sink while Nancy set several dishes on the counter.

"What would you like?" she asked. "We had leftovers for lunch and there's still plenty."

I perused the choices and settled on macaroni and cheese along with a helping of green beans. Seated at the table with the best mac and cheese I'd ever eaten (homemade with a heavenly blend of cheeses melted together), I listened to the two women talk about their plans for dinner and the evening ahead.

"Of course, you'll join us," Nancy said, taking a sip from the cup of tea Charli set in front of her.

"Like I mentioned earlier, I really need to speak with Tim before I agree to anything."

"Give him a call," Nancy said. "One of the boys can stay with the horse. Tim would want to know you're here."

When I didn't immediately take out my phone, Nancy gave me a stern, grandmotherly frown. "Go on, darling. He'll be happy to hear from you."

I had my doubts, but I slid the phone out of my back pocket and dialed Tim's number. We listened as somewhere nearby a ringtone of "Santa Bring My Baby Back to Me" began to play.

Nancy grinned at me as Charli hurried into the laundry room. She returned with the ringing phone in her hand. "Guess Tim forgot his phone when he switched coats earlier. Good thing you came, Carol, or his phone might have gone through a load of wash. He had a little manure incident with a sick calf before breakfast and had to change his clothes."

If Tim's phone had been in the laundry room all morning, then he hadn't even seen my text. As far as he knew, I was still keeping my distance.

Anxious to see him, I shoveled in the last few bites of lunch, drained my cup of tea, and stood. "I think I should go talk to Tim."

"He's in the big barn," Nancy said. I didn't miss the wink she sent Charli as the two women watched me yank on my coat and loop my thick scarf around my neck. I tugged on a pair of mittens and headed toward the door.

"You'll freeze out there. At least wear a hat," Charli said, plopping a big furry thing on my head with flaps that covered my ears. No doubt existed in my mind that I looked ridiculous, but the hat did keep my head warm.

Brutus kept me company as I rushed out to the barn. I gave him a few pats before I opened the door and stepped inside, grateful for the warmth. As my eyes adjusted to the dim interior, I heard Tim's deep rumble and someone answering although I couldn't distinguish their words. I followed the sounds to a stall where Tim and Jack worked to calm a horse that looked like it had been starved and abused.

Careful not to startle any of them, I cautiously moved to the right until I was in Tim's line of sight. He glanced up then did a double take. I'm sure I was the last person he expected to see in the barn, particularly on Christmas Eve.

"I'll be back in a minute, Jack," he said, slowly moving around the horse until he reached me at the stall door. "Hi." The expression on his face was impassive and I had no idea if he was happy to see me or annoyed that I'd shown up out of the blue.

"Hi," I said, wanting to hug him. Exhaustion lined his eyes and he was dirty from the day's adventures, but I couldn't think when I'd seen a better sight than Tim Burke.

"What are you doing here?" he asked, peeling off his glove then placing his hand on my elbow and guiding me toward the door.

"I wanted to talk to you and I had some news to share. I texted you earlier, but Charli found your phone in the laundry room."

He patted his pockets and sighed. "That would explain why my phone has been so quiet all morning." With a glance back at the stall where Jack leaned out of it, watching us, Tim pushed open the door. "Let's talk out there."

Brutus' tail fanned the snow, making an interesting pattern as he sat near the door, waiting for a human to appear.

Tim ruffled the dog's ears, pulled on the glove he'd removed earlier, and motioned for me to walk with him.

"What's up?" he asked, keeping a respectable distance between the two of us. It seemed more like the width of the Grand Canyon.

"Jason called me this morning. They arrested the guy who's been stalking me. I don't have to be afraid anymore, Tim. I wanted you to know that, and to know I'd like to spend time with you again. Now that he's in jail, I don't have to worry about anyone getting hurt because of me."

He stopped walking and frowned at me. "So, the whole needing time thing was really your way of trying to control things? Of trying to keep me safe, in case your crazy stalker dude ever found his way to Montana?"

I nodded, sensing the conversation was not going to go at all like I'd envisioned. I'd pictured Tim elated over the arrest of Curtis, thrilled I wanted to be with him. He'd take me in his arms, kissing me senseless.

One look at the angry set of his jaw confirmed that wasn't going to happen.

Tim scoffed and started walking again. "That's rich, Carol. You were willing to sacrifice the chance at real happiness because of something that might never happen? And now that the threat is gone, you're ready to pick up where we left off?"

When he said it like that, it sounded bad. Made me sound like a twit, which I admittedly had been.

"You don't get to make decisions for other people, in case you weren't aware of the fact. You lied to me and now I'm supposed to just forget all about it? That's not how things work, at least not with me. You wanted time, so now you have all of it in the world you'll ever need. This conversation is finished." Tim started walking faster, heading I knew not where.

Momentarily stunned by his words and his anger, I stood rooted to the spot, feet growing cold in the snow. I could let the best thing that ever happened to me walk away, or I could fight for him, for our love.

My dad hadn't called me tenacious for nothing.

My long legs quickly covered the ground between us. I stepped in front of him, forcing him to stop as I gathered my thoughts.

"I didn't lie," I said, grabbing his arm when he turned away from me. "I did need time away from you, Tim. Every moment I spent with you made me fall more in love and it got harder and harder to think about walking away. I was so worried the man intent on doing me harm would eventually find me here and hurt those I care about. The last person in the world I'd want to hurt is you."

He shook off my hand, crossed his arms over that burly chest, and glared at me. When he didn't say a word, I rushed ahead.

"This is a long story that I'll try to condense, but I couldn't sleep so I got up super early this morning with a strong feeling of unease. When I went into the store, I found Mia McBride asleep in one of the chairs. She'd hid there all night and not told her family. I took her home and as I stood watching her reunite with her father and brother, I realized I can't control the future and I can't linger in the past. I need to live in the present and I'm really, really hoping you're still interested in being part of it. I missed you so much, Tim, and I…" I hesitated to just blurt out my feelings, but today had been a most unusual day. "I love you."

Despite my imploring looks, his face remained devoid of expression. "Look, I know I messed up. I should have been forthright with you instead of backing away from our relationship. I'm sorry, Tim. I'm truly sorry. But I sent you the text asking if we could talk long before Jason called to tell me about Curtis being arrested."

The frown he'd worn since I started talking deepened. "Who's Curtis?"

"The stalker. I dated him when I first moved to New York. He was an intern working for a photographer then. He never knew me as anyone other than Lyra, which is why he hadn't found me here. But he tried to kill Blake, the detective pretending to be me, after breaking into my apartment. He won't be bothering anyone for a long, long time."

His head barely moved up and down in what might have been construed as a nod.

"Tim, I don't know what else to say to you." I threw my hands up in the air. "I was an idiot and a control freak and I regret my actions more than you can possibly know. I'm sorry. So very sorry. If you ever find it in your heart to forgive me, you know where to find me. I guess this is goodbye."

My heart felt like it had been ripped in two and stomped to bits, but I turned away from him and started walking toward the house.

"When are you leaving for New York?" he called after me, his voice sounding rough and pained.

Unwilling to turn around and let Tim see the tears that streamed from my eyes and froze on my cheeks, I kept walking.

"Carol!" he yelled.

I heard the crunch of snow as he hurried to

catch up to me. Without thinking, I broke into a run, focused only on reaching my car and going home.

One minute I was running in the snow, the next I was swept into Tim's arms and held close to his chest.

"Baby, don't cry," he whispered, kissing my cold cheeks. "Please don't cry."

"I'm not going back to New York," I said between sniffles.

Tim's head shot up in surprise. "Say that again."

I took a calming breath and looked up at him, at the face I so dearly loved. "I'm not going back to New York. I told Jason it was time for Lyra to retire. We'll discuss the particulars in January. My home is here." I placed my hand over his heart, hoping he understood I meant not just Christmas Mountain, but with him.

"I love you, Carol. So, so much," he said and lowered his head to mine.

The sweet kiss he pressed to my lips soon turned into something more. Electric sparks sizzled and popped between us as passion and hunger infused the exchange.

The sound of cheers and clapping finally penetrated the feeling we were the only two humans in the world. My face turned red as we looked over by the barn to see Jack, the ranch hands, Charli, and even the vet watching us.

"It's about time someone made you fall big time, Tim," Jack hollered, waving his hat at him.

Tim chuckled and fell back in the snow while I yelled "Timber!"

We might have stayed there, keeping each other warm with tempting kisses if Brutus hadn't bounded over and demanded attention. We got to our feet and let the dog know he wasn't being ignored then headed back to the house.

# *Epilogue*

I stood next to Joy off to the side of the stage in the community center on Christmas night, prepared to sing in tribute to Ms. King. All our friends were there with us: Ashley, Morgan, Emma, Faith, and Lexi.

Although she didn't say anything, I knew Joy was nervous. She was a fabulous piano player, but it wasn't until her fingers touched the keys that her anxiety fell away.

I was a little nervous, too. I'd peeked out at the audience and saw Tim there with Nancy, Charli, and Jack. Seated next to them was Mia McBride with her father and brother. My heart swelled to see them all there.

When it was our turn to take the stage, I nudged

Joy and we walked out. The notes rang out clear and true from the old piano Steve, Joy's neighbor and current love interest, had repaired. The community center still had a way to go in being restored to its former glory, but I intended to help it get there.

In no time at all, our song was at an end and we bowed, leaving the stage. After the show, I hurried out to find Tim. Mia ran up to me and engulfed me in an enthusiastic hug.

"Thank you for making today wonderful, Carol."

"It was Santa and his elves," I teased, returning her hug, then shaking her father's hand and smiling at her brother.

"We owe you, Miss Bennett," Mr. McBride said. "Anytime you need anything from us, all you have to do is ask."

I nodded. "I appreciate that, sir. The only thing I'll ask right now is that you spend some time becoming a family again."

He nodded and wrapped an arm around Mia's shoulder then kissed the top of her head. "We'll definitely do that."

Before I could say anything further, I felt a warm presence behind me and turned as Tim wrapped me in his arms. His cowboy hat, held in his left hand, bumped against my back as he gave me a hug.

"You sang like an angel," he whispered in my ear as he bent his head close to mine. "You look like one, too."

I'd taken extra care with my appearance,

curling my hair, applying makeup, and wearing a sapphire blue dress a designer had created just for me. It always made me feel like a million bucks to wear it and from the appreciative glances Tim cast my way, he liked it, too.

"You don't look so bad yourself," I said, leaning back just enough to take in the way his broad shoulders filled out his suit jacket, western-cut, of course. "In fact, I think you're the most handsome cowboy I've ever seen and that includes all the ones I've watched in all those old John Wayne movies."

He grinned and my heart tripped in my chest. "How about we go back to your place and watch one of those movies?"

"I'd be up for that," I said, not caring what we did as long as we were together. He went with me to get my coat and held it while I slipped it on. After I said my goodbyes to my friends and his family, we stepped outside into the crisp December air.

Tim looked down at me with a tender smile. "I'm making a promise to you, my beautiful Christmas Carol."

"What's that?" I asked, unable to think of anything that would make me any happier in that moment than being with Tim. His love was all I needed or wanted.

"If I never do anything else for the rest of my life, I'm gonna love you, Carol Bennett, with every bit of my heart. You mean the world to me."

I reached up and nudged his head toward mine, until our lips were almost touching. "You mean everything to me and then some. Come on, cowboy, let's go home."

Only when Tim's hand firmly clasped mine did we head toward my store, ready to walk into a future together, one filled with hope and so much love.

If you enjoyed spending time with these characters,
I hope you'll read Lacey's story in

Christmas Mountain Clean Romance Series
Book 8
*Pre-order it today!*

~*~

Thank you for reading *Between Christmas and Romance*. I hope you enjoyed meeting Carol and Tim and reading their story. If you have just a moment, would you please leave a <u>review</u> so others might discover this book? I'd so appreciate it!

If you haven't read them, please check out my other holiday books in the _Rodeo Romance_, _Hardman Holidays_, and _Friendly Beasts of Faraday_ series!

Also, if you haven't yet signed up for my newsletter, won't you consider subscribing? I send it out when I have new releases, sales, or news of freebies to share. Each month, you can enter a contest, get a new recipe to try, and discover details about upcoming events. When you sign up, you'll receive a free digital book. Don't wait. Sign up today!

_Shanna's Newsletter_

And if newsletters aren't your thing, please follow me on BookBub.

You'll receive notifications on pre-orders, new releases, and sale books!

_BookBub_

# *Recipe*

Although Aunt Charli would undoubtedly make the entire cake from scratch, here is a quick and easy version of her spice cake. It's moist, full of flavor, and so good on a cold winter day!

### *Spice Bundt Cake*

Ingredients:
### *Cake*
1 box vanilla cake mix
1 small package instant white chocolate pudding
1 teaspoon vanilla extract
1 cup sour cream
1/2 cup water
1/2 cup oil
3 eggs
2 tablespoons cinnamon
1 teaspoon ginger
2 teaspoons nutmeg
### *Butter Sauce*
1/2 cup butter
1/2 cup heavy cream
1 cup packed brown sugar
1 tablespoon vanilla extract

Directions:
*Note:* If desired, you can purchase a spice cake mix and omit the additional spices.

Preheat oven to 350 degrees.

In a large bowl, beat eggs until lightly mixed. Add water, vanilla, oil and sour cream and mix on low speed until blended then add cake batter and pudding and mix on medium speed. Add in spices. Beat until combined. The batter will be super thick, so don't panic.

Scoop it into a greased bundt pan, evening it up as best you can. Bake for approximately one hour or until it starts to pull away from the edges of the pan.

Let cool completely then invert on a cake plate.

To make the sauce, combine butter, cream and sugar in saucepan. Bring to a boil, stirring consistently, then reduce and simmer for about 10 minutes or until sauce thickens. Add vanilla, stirring well. Cool slightly then drizzle over cake.

Serve with ice cream or cinnamon-laced whipped cream. Yum!

## *Author's Note*

Happy holidays, dear reader! I'm so glad you've taken this little journey with me to Christmas Mountain. Wouldn't it be a fun place to visit if it truly existed? I'd love to go there and hang out at Rudolph's Reads with Carol and maybe spend the day at the ranch or indulge in one of Aunt Charli's meals.

There are just a few little things I thought I'd share that inspired details in this story.

When I was asked to join this series, the character names were already established. Every time I saw Carol Bennett's name, it made me giggle and think of Carol Burnett. Maybe that's why I chose her! And it was easy to have Tim needle her about her name when they first met. The day I was sharing with Captain Cavedweller about her name and how I planned to have him mix it up on purpose, he thought I should give the hero a name she could make fun of, too, and suggested Tim Burke. It was perfect!

The scene where Carol is trying to exercise and rolls over to find a pair of feline eyeballs unsettlingly close to hers happened to me one morning with our loony cat. If you've ever tried to do crunches while keeping an attention-hungry cat at bay, you know just what I mean when I had Carol give up exercising and pet her cat instead. Hemi, like our whackadoodle feline, can be a loveable pest at times (okay, most of the time!).

You may have gathered from the story that Carol has a thing for tea. I love tea! It's so delicious and comforting on a cold winter day and there are so, so many flavors of it to enjoy. One of my favorites for the holiday season is Nutcracker Sweet from Celestial Seasonings.

I grew up near a small town and it was fun to write about the people of Christmas Mountain coming together to give the McBride family a special Christmas. I could casily picture some people I know doing the same thing.

Thank you, again, for reading *Between Christmas and Romance*.

Wishing you and yours a beautiful holiday season!

Hopeless romantic Shanna Hatfield spent ten years as a newspaper journalist before moving into the field of marketing and public relations. Sharing the romantic stories she dreams up in her head is a perfect outlet for her love of writing, reading, and creativity. She and her husband, lovingly referred to as Captain Cavedweller, reside in the Pacific Northwest.

Shanna loves to hear from readers. Connect with her online:
Blog: shannahatfield.com
Facebook: Shanna Hatfield's Page
Shanna Hatfield's Hopeless Romantics Group
Pinterest: Shanna Hatfield
Email: shanna@shannahatfield.com